THE WOLVES OF CRAYWOOD

Dark tragedy strikes the three Cray brothers: two girls have been brutally torn apart by vicious beasts — the countryside around Craywood blazes with the legends of the werewolf. No one believes that a man could have caused such horror . . . Gaye reluctantly answers her sister Susan's call for help and learns that Susan blames Walter Cray for the killings. Nightmare follows nightmare, and soon Gaye herself is marked for death! Can anyone stop *The Wolves of Craywood*?

V. J. BANIS

THE WOLVES OF CRAYWOOD

Complete and Unabridged

LINFORD
Leicester

First published in Great Britain

First Linford Edition
published 2012

British Library CIP Data

Banis, Victor J.
 The wolves of Craywood. - -
 (Linford mystery library)
 1. Suspense fiction.
 2. Large type books.
 I. Title II. Series
 813.5'4–dc23

 ISBN 978–1–4448–1076–9

Published by
F. A. Thorpe (Publishing)
Anstey, Leicestershire

Set by Words & Graphics Ltd.
Anstey, Leicestershire
Printed and bound in Great Britain by
T. J. International Ltd., Padstow, Cornwall

This book is printed on acid-free paper

Prologue

It had always frightened her to be in the woods at night alone. Now, however, she was not alone, and it was this realization that sent little shivers of fear dancing up and down the back of her neck.

I should have gone home by the road, she thought, chewing her lip, but the shortcut through the woods saved ten minutes, ten minutes longer to spend with him — and she had used the shortcut before, without any problems.

Maybe, she thought, she had imagined it — but as though in reply to that thought, a twig snapped somewhere nearby. She peered into the darkness, ears straining. An animal, probably. But what kind of animal?

There was a sound of movement in the brush nearby.

Just to her left was the wood that lay between her and home, still a good half mile away. To her right, an open field stretched a few hundred yards to the fence of Spencer's orchard, and beyond that she could see the lights from the Spencer house. If she yelled, they would probably hear her, even from here. To cross the field, however, was to walk in moonlight, with no shelter and no place to hide, while in the thick darkness of the woods she might be able to get away from . . . *from what?*

She began to walk into the field, toward the distant light that flickered through the branches of the trees. Incongruously she thought how sweet the clover smelled. The tall grass swished against her legs and tugged at the hem of her skirt.

There was a crashing of brush behind her. She glanced back once, long enough to see one shadow, blacker than the others, bounding swiftly toward her. As she began to run, she tried to scream, but all that came out was a muffled, gurgling sound. The grass stung her legs. Something, a fallen stick, probably, struck sharply against her right knee, almost making her fall.

Now there were other noises pursuing her. She could hear breathing, sounding horribly near, and strange grunting sounds, like snarls. She couldn't look and she couldn't find her voice to cry out. Tears began to stream from her eyes, running in chill streams over her cheeks.

She ran into a rut. Her foot twisted and suddenly she was tumbling into the tall, coarse weeds. She rolled and it seemed she was falling up, into the sky. Suddenly the sky was gone. She screamed once, a shrill, eerie sound that sped up into the night and raced over the treetops of Spencer's apple orchard.

★ ★ ★

Ben Spencer turned abruptly from the television screen, toward the open door. His wife saw the move and looked from the door to her husband.

'What's the matter?' she asked.

'Thought I heard something.' He got up and went to the door, flicking on the porch light. It made the screen door look like silvery gauze. Beyond the light, everything appeared normal and still.

His wife came to stand beside him. 'I didn't hear anything,' she said, looking past his shoulder.

They listened, but there was only the sound of a nearby cricket gnashing his legs. Ben flicked off the light and started to turn from the door.

Another sound arrested him. This one was louder, more distinct — a long keen wail that went beyond the ear, to tingle the very marrow in the bones. It arched upward, floating high and far, and then paled to a whisper and was ended.

Annie Spencer's hand went instinctively to her throat. She looked at her husband with wide eyes. 'What was that?' she asked.

For a moment Ben stared and listened. 'It sounded like a wolf,' he said finally.

'There ain't any wolves around here.'

It came again, further away and not so loud. It lasted only a few seconds, but it left an after-sound that hovered in the darkness.

Ben closed the door. Annie saw that he locked and bolted it, which they did very rarely. He went back to his chair in front of the television.

'It sounded like a wolf,' he said again.

* * *

Turkey Stoddard ran like a demon through the tall grass. In his hand he clenched a long blue neck scarf, such as girls sometimes wear. He did not need the moonlight to tell him that it and his hands were drenched with blood, still wet and warm.

Horror and revulsion ran with him.

1

The road seemed interminable. Gaye Hanson guided her Chevy cautiously around a sharp curve and wished she were back in Los Angeles, hundreds of miles to the south, in her comfortable little apartment. She was tired. She had been driving all day and all evening. It was odd that after so many years and so much bitterness, she should have responded so quickly and so unquestioningly to Susan's call. Sisterly love? Gaye smiled to herself. Being an old fashioned girl, as Susan had always caustically described her, did have its inconveniences.

Of course it was more than that. The sound of Susan's voice, when she first recognized it on the phone, had unnerved her, but its tone as Susan talked had genuinely frightened her. She had not had to forgive Susan — that was Susan's first question — she had long since done that. At least, if she had never mentally

7

formed the words, I forgive you, Susan, at least she had stopped hurting and stopped resenting, and that was very nearly the same thing.

Susan was frightened, though, and she imparted that fear as much by what she did not say as by what she did. 'I can't explain it to you now, on the phone, but you mustn't let them know this was a put up thing. I'll tell them you're just coming to pay a belated sisterly visit.'

Gaye took the next curve faster, a little too fast perhaps, and as the road climbed straight ahead for a distance, she pushed down on the accelerator. Surely she must be almost there, but beyond the probing headlights was nothing but solid darkness.

What happened next was so sudden, and she so tired, that she scarcely comprehended at all. There was a movement before her, dimming for a second the flow of the lights. Normally a good driver, she reacted without thinking. She jerked the wheel to the right and hit the brakes hard. The rear end broke loose in the gravel and she careened out of control, into the gully at the side of the road. The car crashed to a stop on some boulders, slamming her painfully against the steering wheel.

She sat for a moment in dazed silence. Then, gingerly, she moved her head, her hands, her feet. Everything seemed functional, if a bit shaky. Everything, that was, except the car. It refused to move at all.

'Oh.' She remembered suddenly the figure — it was a man, surely, it had been so unexpected — who had darted in front of her on the road. Had she hit him? And here she was, worrying about a stupid car.

She clambered out quickly, stumbling on a rock, and climbed up to the road. Somehow her headlights had gone off. A thick darkness surrounded the car.

'Hello,' she called up the road. No answer came back to her. She started walking, following the car's tracks in the gravel. How far had she skidded, anyway? It had seemed to go on forever, but it could only have involved seconds.

She saw him as he climbed to his feet, scarcely more than another shadow. Had he not moved she would not have seen him at all. As it was, he was in sight for only a second before he ran, loped, really, doubled over as if in pain, and disappeared into the forest of pine that bordered the road.

'Wait,' she called after him, and began to run. She had hit him, then, hard enough to knock him down — but why had he run from her like that, unless he were stunned and not thinking clearly? 'Wait.'

She went into the woods after him, thinking only that she must see if he were all right. After a few feet, she paused, but then she saw him kneeling some yards ahead. She hurried toward him, but it wasn't him at all, it was a long-ago-fallen tree.

There was a sudden cry from somewhere in the darkness of the forest, not a human cry, but wild, like the howl of a wolf. It made her skin tingle. She turned around slowly, and for the first time, she thought how reckless she had been to plunge into the woods after someone, or *something*. No, it had been a man, she was certain of that. As for wolves, she didn't believe they had them here, not even in California's northernmost reaches.

The night air was sweet with the scent of pine and juniper and sage. What had seemed to be silence was not silence at all. The leaves and boughs sighed in a breeze, and there were winged creatures who whispered overheard — and a faint rustling sound that could have been the breeze again moving through the thick growth, or it could have been someone moving cautiously, off to her right there, where a branch moved too suddenly — or did it?

She was not easily frightened, but she was frightened now. She turned back toward the car, but there was a pine tree in her way that shouldn't have been there. She had come from the road in a straight path. She moved to the left to go about the tree, and found her way blocked by a thick bush. She stopped short and looked about her. Here in the woods the darkness was even more complete. She could not even see where the road was. Somehow she had gotten turned about.

She jumped when the wail came again,

scattering the night sounds before it, but it sounded further away. If it were a wolf — which it could not be — then it wasn't tracking her, at least. *Chances are,* she thought, *it's some stray dog shivering in his tracks because he heard me.*

Another sound intruded upon the night, the sound of an automobile engine coming to life. It faded for a second and then roared again as it mounted some rise. In a moment she saw the lights. They came and went and came again between the trees as the car snaked its way up the twisting road. Now she could hear more clearly the deep-throated snarl of the car's engine as it voiced its mastery of the steep climb. The lights became two and distinct, seemed about to sweep over her, dipped and veered instead. She had a glimpse of red before the darkness closed in about her again. The road was no more than twenty feet away, past that tree in front of her. She circled it and moved cautiously in that direction.

There was a sound of hard braking, a scattering of gravel as the car came to an abrupt stop a short distance up the road.

12

Its continuing growl helped guide her and a minute later she was out of the bushes and standing in gravel and a settling cloud of dust. Up the road, in the glare of headlights, her car leaned precariously to one side. Behind it was the red car that had just passed, its taillights gleaming, its door open. It was a Ferrari. Her boss in Los Angeles had driven one. It was, she knew, extremely high-powered, and extremely expensive.

Someone crossed through the path of the lights, around to the open door on the driver's side. A man paused, silhouetted, watching Gaye approach hurriedly.

'Am I glad to see you,' she said in way of introduction, and she was, too. If he had been Jack the Ripper, he would still have been preferable to the chilling fear she had felt in the woods a moment before, when that animal, whatever it had been, had howled.

The light was behind the stranger, so she still could not see him clearly. She had an impression of a very powerful body. He was tall, certainly, thick in the shoulders and neck, and slim-waisted.

13

'Is that your car?' a deep baritone asked.

'Yes.' She paused, aware that he was staring hard at her, she supposed because she had come out of the woods. 'Something ran in front of me,' she said. 'I forgot about the loose gravel and braked too suddenly.'

He pulled his eyes away from her and nodded in the direction of her car. 'Will it run?'

'It acted hung up.'

He went back around the Ferrari again, to the Chevy, and bent down to look underneath. Gaye found herself looking not at her car but at the broad back with its thick muscles straining against a fitted silk shirt.

'Bent the radius rod,' the stranger announced. 'And severed a king pin.'

'Translated into English, that means . . . ?'

'I could probably straighten the rod, but the king pin is bad news.'

He stood, dusting his hands as he did so. He turned toward Gaye and for the first time she saw the man in the full spread of light. It took only a single glance to tell her this was easily the

14

handsomest man she had ever seen — and working for a photo news magazine, she had seen a few. His hair was blond, bleached by the same sun that had turned the smooth skin bronze. His eyebrows were thick and untrained, and long, almost feminine lashes shaded eyes so blue they were surely indecent.

One corner of his full mouth lifted ever so slightly. She blushed, realizing that she was staring.

'You'll have to leave it here,' he went on. 'Until you can get a tow truck up here. Not a chance of that before morning, I'm afraid. The nearest one is twenty miles off, and you won't get old Miller out of bed at this hour.'

'Darn.' In her disappointment she even forgot her companion's good looks.

'Can I give you a lift?' he asked. 'There's a motel about thirty miles back, on the main road. Nothing great, but it's not the Bates, either.'

His voice contained an unasked question: both cars were pointed in the other direction, further up into the mountains.

'I was on my way to a place called

Craywood,' she said. 'I think it's another couple of miles. If you're going that far, I'd appreciate the lift.'

She thought one pale eyebrow tilted upward, but his expression remained too impassive to be certain.

'I can take you right to the door, as a matter of fact,' was what he said. 'Where's your luggage?' He seemed to think it was settled.

Well, my dear, don't look a gift horse in the mouth, she told herself. She got her bag out of the Chevy. He took it from her and put it neatly behind his seat. By the time she got her purse, he was waiting behind the wheel of the Ferrari.

She was scarcely in before they were moving. As she slammed the door, he sent the powerful car shooting forward, veering effortlessly and gracefully about the Chevy and hurtling up the hill with a loud roar. Gaye's eyes widened as a curve rushed toward them. They took it with scarcely any lessening of speed, but sure and flat. She let out the breath she had sucked in. The man drove as well as he looked.

As if he read her thoughts, he said, 'I drive Monte Carlo every year, and the race at Le Mans two years ago. This road is tame in comparison.'

A quick downshift and another curve whipped past, while the engine growled with acceleration. Gaye grinned, her spirits accelerating too. A youthful excitement gripped her. Speed alone did not scare her, not when combined with a skilled driver. The windows were open, and the night wind disarranged her dark hair playfully.

'Do you know the people at Craywood?' the stranger asked.

She hesitated, wondering how much to tell. Susan had been so secretive on the phone. 'Only Susan Hanson,' she said. 'I'm sorry, Susan Cray it is now. Do you know her?'

He ignored the question and asked, instead, 'You don't know the Cray family, then?'

'I've heard of them, of course.' Not a lie, exactly, although it was skirting the truth, but it was hardly the sort of truth one would want to discuss with a stranger, and even a little of the story would require more just to make it clear.

'Oh? What have you heard?'

She laughed softly to herself. For a moment there she had felt the faintest tinge of the old bitterness. How many nights had she cried herself to sleep with the name Cray on her lips? Aloud, she said, 'Very little. There are two brothers, one an aging lecher — that would be Susan's husband — and the other a dilettante playboy.'

'Your friend Susan told you that?'

'Some of it came from other sources.'

'Really? I'm sorry we haven't time to discuss your sources. They sound intriguing.'

'They . . . ' She paused as his inference became clear. 'Oh, are we . . . ?'

She did not get to finish her question. They turned suddenly and hard, drifting while the engine shrieked and the tires clawed and massive gateposts swept by. High walls and higher trees had hidden the approaching house from view. Now, as they shot up a sweeping driveway, there it was before them, a massive structure, perhaps four stories high, jutting out in every direction and at every angle. At first glimpse, it was as awesome as it was ugly.

It grew, filling her field of vision and then they skidded to a stop at the front steps where lights gleamed on thick, Doric columns. The windows were bright. Despite all her misgivings, Gaye thought it looked very welcoming after the long trip.

'Craywood,' the man behind the wheel said, indicating the house with a sweep of his hand. 'Home of lechers, dilettantes and your friend, Susan.'

'Goodness, I didn't expect service to the door,' Gaye said, pulling her eyes from the house to look at her rescuer. 'But I certainly appreciate it more than I can say, Mister . . . ?' She put out her hand.

He took it, shaking it as firmly as though it were a man's.

'Cray,' he said, 'Carlton Cray.' To Gaye's stunned expression, he added, 'I'm the dilettante playboy. My brother is the lecher.'

2

It was the sort of situation not covered by Emily Post. Carlton Cray left her standing foolishly by the car, went swiftly up the steps, and threw the door open. It crashed against a wall and he left it standing wide.

Dear Miss Post, do I follow my recently insulted host inside? Or do I stand penitently outside and ring the bell in the hope that someone will give me permission to come in? Or do I walk back to the road and wait for another car to come along, in front of which to fling myself?

Susan solved the problem for her while Gaye hesitated on the steps. The crashing of the door brought Susan into the wide front hall, into the path of the angry man.

'Carlton,' Susan said, looking surprised as he strode quickly by her. She saw Gaye outside and looked even more surprised. 'Gaye. Did you two come together?'

'I had an accident on the road,' Gaye explained lamely, coming into the bright hall. 'Mister Cray luckily came by in time to give me a lift up here. I'm afraid I didn't endear myself, though.'

'Don't feel badly,' Susan said with a little grimace. 'With Carlton, no one does.'

Carlton Cray had disappeared into one of the rooms opening off the hall. For a long moment, Susan and Gaye were silent, staring at one another, taking inventory. It was five years since they had last seen one another. Gaye did not know how much she herself had changed in that time, but her sister had changed quite a bit.

Susan was still lovely, of course. Gaye had always envied her blonde elegance. At nineteen, Gaye had been the dark haired, rather ordinary looking younger sister, and even then she'd had that aura of self-possession that discouraged any man not equally self-possessed. Susan, two years older, had been the raving beauty, reeking of femininity and charm, and bringing out in just about every man whatever it was that made him want to hold someone small and helpless in his arms and protect and comfort her.

Helpless? Well, that was the way Susan played it, and even knowing better, as Gaye certainly did, it was still easy to think of her that way. It was in the very air she breathed, you could not help being captured by that illusion — for a time, at least.

Then how had she changed? It was strange that Gaye could not pinpoint exactly what it was that was different. Susan had changed, though, and it was more than the tiny lines which she had tried very bravely to conceal at the corners of her eyes, lines that oughtn't to be there at twenty-six, and more than the cold lips frozen now in a nervous smile. Gaye thought fleetingly that whatever inner light had made Susan's eyes gleam and her skin glow had gone out.

She opened her arms in the old gesture, however, and Susan came into them, embracing her gently at first and then hugging her as fiercely as she used to do.

'Oh, Gaye, I'm so glad you're here,' she said. She put her blonde head on Gaye's shoulder — the old gesture, helpless and in need of protection.

'I'm glad to be here,' Gaye said. She prevented herself from adding, *at last. So this*, she thought, her eyes going beyond Susan's blonde hair to view the monstrous hall, *this is Craywood. This is where I might have lived these five years, if . . .*

'Hello, Gaye.'

She had not heard Walter Cray come into the hall, and at the sound of his voice, so shockingly familiar after all this time, she stiffened. So many times she had thought of this moment, wondering if such a meeting would ever take place, and if so, what it would be like. On the long drive here, knowing that at last it was going to happen, she had rehearsed over and over in her mind just how it would be, but it was like the plunge into an icy pool of water — no matter how you prepared yourself for it, it was still a shock.

She moved out of Susan's embrace and

turned toward him. 'Hello, Walter,' she said evenly. She saw him, and it was all right.

The years had not been kind to Walter. He was still handsome, his eyes still caught and held one's gaze with the old charm, his smile was still the same flashing thing it had been.

It was different now, though. He was ten years her senior. The gap might have been twenty. His changed hairstyle did not conceal the receding hairline as it was obviously intended to do. Years of drinking too heavily and eating too heavily and exercising too lightly had left deep shadows about his eyes, a puffiness that distorted his once lean face, and a bloated figure.

It was not really the physical changes that mattered so much. A woman in love does not put so much store on the physical as does a man in the same frame of mind. And that, really, was what it came down to: she no longer loved him. She had thought not, had believed that she was over that girlish crush, but still there had lingered the question.

Now it was answered. He meant nothing to her. He was a badly aging man who had once been, briefly, the object of her love, her first and only one, and who had thrown her over for her more beautiful sister.

'You are as lovely as ever,' he said, taking her hands in his own.

'And you are as fast with the phrase as ever,' she replied, but without malice.

'I was so pleasantly surprised when Susan said you had called. You changed jobs, she said.'

'That's putting it tactfully. *Photo World* folded, leaving Gaye Hanson, staff writer, out of a job. I took a much needed vacation. I've been rambling around Mexico for the last few weeks, and I decided before I started into the routine again, I ought to pay a visit up here. So . . . ' She shrugged her shoulders.

'Hasn't anyone offered our guest a drink?' Carlton Cray emerged from one of the rooms off the hall. He held a brandy in his hand and smiled sardonically. Gaye put a hand to her face, surprised to discover there was no egg there.

'You've met my brother Carlton,' Walter said without looking in his brother's direction.

'Miss Hanson and I have had the pleasure, although I'm afraid we were both a little less than candid with one another.'

He spoke directly to Gaye, and though his tone was cutting, there was something like genuine amusement in his eyes. She thought it would be very difficult to be angry with this man for any length of time.

Susan, however, apparently suffered no such difficulty. 'I had hoped we'd have time to prepare you for Carlton,' she said. 'He takes some getting used to.'

'But I can assure you, your sister and I got along quite well,' Carlton said. 'She seemed not to notice the lack of charm with which you both fault me.'

'Mister Cray was very kind,' Gaye said, heading off the quarrel that was looming. 'Were it not for him I might still be trudging along the road out there.'

She saw Carlton's gaze flit from her to Walter and back to her, and she knew what he must be thinking of. For some reason she felt a blush of embarrassment that he should know about her and Walter, and that Walter had jilted her, but at the same time she was relieved that he did know. She would not want to try to deceive those intense eyes that sparkled at her when he smiled.

'I believe I could use a drink,' she said. 'It's been an awfully long day.'

'Of course,' Walter said. 'Susan, take your sister into the den. I'll go find Louise and ask her to bring us a bite to eat.'

He left them. Gaye followed Susan past Carlton, into a large paneled room. Although it was summer, they were in the mountains and the night was cool. A fire burned low in the fireplace. The ceilings were high and beamed.

'What would you like?' Susan asked.

'A brandy,' Gaye said. When Susan brought it, she took a sip, its warming glow reminding her of how tired she was.

Carlton remained in the doorway, merely turning to face into the room. 'Where's my brother?' he asked after a moment.

It was an odd question, Gaye thought. Walter had left them only a moment before.

'In his room,' Susan said. 'He's not been well.'

'Walter didn't tell me.'

Susan looked surprised by the remark. 'Have you talked to him?' she asked — too quickly, Gaye thought, although the exchange made no sense to her.

Carlton thought the question too quick also. His frozen smile came back. 'You mean you haven't gotten around to tapping the phones yet?' he asked.

Susan's look was one of pure hatred. Gaye, remembering Susan's temper, wondered if Carlton Cray knew what sort of fire he was playing with.

The exchange was cut short by an abrupt arrival. There came a whirring and clicking from the hall and a moment later a young man in a wheelchair suddenly filled the doorway.

He was very young, no more than twenty, Gaye would have guessed, and good looking, although handsome was not the exact term that sprang to mind.

He was what would once have been described as tragically beautiful, a blend of Carlton's handsomeness and Walter's flair. From the waist up he seemed to possess a splendid physique. He wore a polo shirt and it showed off a thick chest and firmly muscled arms, but the plaid blanket that covered him from the waist down could not fully conceal the twisted shapes beneath.

'Hello, Carlton,' he said with only the faintest glimmer of cheerfulness. Even that vanished when his eyes passed over Susan without pause and settled on Gaye. 'Good evening,' he said, and his voice sounded incredibly old and quite unsuited to his youthful appearance. 'I'm Dennis Cray, the younger brother.'

Gaye was completely unprepared for the arrival of Dennis Cray or for the announcement, and that was how the statement had been delivered, like an announcement.

'Hello,' was all she could think to say.

The young man smiled but there was nothing amiable about his expression. 'I see Walter neglected to mention me.'

'But of course he did,' Gaye lied. It was

not successful. Her lies never were. The young man saw through it and smiled more broadly. So did Carlton.

'This is Miss Hanson, sister to our beloved Susan,' Carlton said. 'Perhaps she'll be kind enough to let us call her Gaye, a charming name, don't you think? This is my brother. Gaye Hanson, Dennis Cray. Walter has always been somewhat embarrassed over Dennis, so you mustn't feel badly about not knowing.'

'How do you do,' Gaye said, taking Dennis's hand in hers briefly. She was uncomfortable under his cold gaze and still embarrassed. She was not sorry when he absented himself a moment later.

'I must get back to my room,' he said. 'I only wanted to welcome you to Craywood, Miss Hanson. We have few visitors and none quite so lovely. Carlton, will you come down and keep me company for a while?'

'Of course.' Carlton made a little bow to Gaye. 'I too welcome you to Craywood. I expect after your trip you will be turning in early, but in the morning we will get better acquainted.'

It was not an invitation, merely a statement of fact. 'Yes,' Gaye said, 'I suppose we will.' He left in Dennis's wake.

Susan was drinking vodka. In the past, Gaye recalled, she had mixed it, but now she was drinking it neat, on the rocks. She stared coldly after Carlton for a moment and then emptied her glass in one long draught.

'I gather you two aren't very friendly,' Gaye said, breaking the silence that had descended.

'That's the understatement of the year,' Susan replied. 'But he's not here often, he's usually travelling around somewhere.'

What she did not say was the question that was plainly bothering her, even if Gaye didn't know what it was all about. Why was Carlton here now? Was it just coincidence? Susan had called her and urgently pleaded with her to come here, and Carlton had shown up at the same time.

For the moment they were alone, and Gaye reminded herself that she was here because of that urgent call. 'What's wrong, Susan?' she asked bluntly.

Susan gave her an odd look. When she spoke, it was as though the question had not been asked. 'Your car's back along the road?' she asked instead.

'Yes. Someone will have to look at it. Carlton thought it would have to be towed.' She was sure Susan was stalling. That was not a new habit, but did it have some added significance here? Was Carlton listening, or Walter? Carlton had made that sarcastic remark about tapping wires — did they spy on one another in this big, cold house, and if they did, why?

'There's a garage in town,' Susan said. 'In the morning we'll ask them to take care of it.'

She looked hard at her empty glass, obviously considering a refill, but Walter came in just then, effusive, telling them that supper was ready.

At the table, Walter kept a flow of talk going so that it seemed they were engaged in conversation, but for the most part, it was nothing more than replies from Susan and Gaye to his stream of questions and comments.

They ate a warm stew and large hunks of fresh bread. The food was served by a gaunt woman whom Walter called Louise. She had a deeply lined face, and a dark complexion, her glossy black hair pulled severely back from her face. Her eyes were narrow and Gaye noticed that she did not look directly at any of them while she served. She gave Gaye the impression that she was angry or frightened, but Gaye was very tired now and it was possible her imagination was working overtime.

'Is she Indian?' Gaye asked when Louise had gone out.

'Mrs. Stoddard is Cajun,' Walter said.

'Louisiana bayou,' Susan added in the way of explanation.

When Louise came to clear away, Gaye saw that she wore a silver crucifix. It was shiny and gleaming and looked perfectly new. She had a strange scent about her, too, that Gaye could not identify. Herbs of some sort, she thought, but that was hardly surprising. The woman was a cook, and of course she would work with herbs.

'I'll show you to your room,' Susan said finally.

Gaye was only too happy. She said good night to Walter and followed Susan down the long central hall, around a corner and down still another hall, this one leading apparently into one of the wings of the house. Both halls were lined with doors. Gaye couldn't begin to guess how many rooms the house must contain. Susan might have told her at some time, it was the sort of thing Susan would have been certain to mention, but if she had, the knowledge had faded from Gaye's memory.

Before, when they shared an apartment in Los Angeles, she and Susan shared one tiny bedroom, a kitchen that would not accommodate both of them at the same time, and an even smaller bathroom. The distance that Susan had come measured far more than what was shown on the map.

It was a relief to Gaye to discover that she did not like Craywood. For all its spaciousness and obvious worth, it was an ugly house, old and gloomy and ill-fitted.

She would never have been happy here, no matter how differently things might have worked out.

Her bedroom was large, high-ceilinged and crowded with massive furniture. Her bed was high enough to require a step at its side to help her get into it. One side of the room was shuttered doors. Gaye went to them and looked upon a flagstone terrace that led to a wall of trees. The woods came literally to the edge of the terrace. They looked dark and ominous. Fleetingly she remembered that unpleasant moment in the darkness of the woods earlier. She had not told anyone of that and now, after this time, she wondered how much of it she had imagined. Certainly she had been in no real danger, despite her fears.

Susan seated herself in one of the two overstuffed chairs in the corner. She smoked a cigarette, looking very nervous.

Gaye sat down on one edge of the huge bed. 'Now, then,' she said in a firm voice. She was tired and would have liked to sleep, but she had not come all this way just to get a good night's sleep. 'Tell me what this is all about.'

Susan hesitated for a long moment, until Gaye thought she would have to pry the truth out of her, but finally Susan stubbed out her cigarette. 'I want to leave Craywood,' she said in a clipped tone.

Gaye felt a little deflated. From Susan's voice on the phone, and her cryptic remarks, she had imagined something more serious than domestic restlessness.

'But that's very simple, isn't it?' she said. 'Why don't you drive down to San Francisco? Or come to Los Angeles with me for a few days. Are you and Walter quarrelling?'

Susan gave her a peculiar look. She seemed to have sensed Gaye's disappointment. She shook her head impatiently. 'Walter won't let me go. He's very possessive.'

Gaye shrugged and thought that after all she would get to bed early. 'Well,' she said, 'I have no right to interfere in your private quarrels, of course, but it seems to me he could hardly keep you from going if you really meant to. After all, you're his wife, that's true, but this is the twentieth century and that no longer implies slavehood. And you're not a child, or mentally incompetent.'

'He would kill me first. He told me as much.'

Gaye laughed and got up from the bed. The room was close. She went to the shuttered doors and opened one of them to the terrace. A gust of night air raced through the room.

'It sounds to me like you're overplaying a domestic quarrel,' she said, turning back to her sister. 'I can't imagine Walter said that in so many words, and even if he did, it was only in the heat of the argument. I may not know Walter as well as you do, but I certainly know him well enough to know that he's not a murderous man.'

She got a shock when Susan looked up at her, directly into her eyes. Susan was serious, dead serious, and she was genuinely frightened. Gaye knew her sister well enough to know when she was pretending or dramatizing, both of which she was prone to do, but this was real, and so blatant that it sent a cold chill up

Gaye's spine. Without turning, without even realizing she did so, she reached behind her to push the door shut again.

'Isn't he?' Susan asked.

'Is he?' Gaye replied in a small voice.

Susan looked away and got another cigarette, lighting it with shaking hands. After a long pause, she said, 'He's already killed twice, you see.'

3

It was difficult to know how to respond to such a remark. For a long moment Gaye could think of nothing to say. Finally she came to sit in the chair beside Susan's. Instinctively she leaned toward her sister and when she spoke, it was in a lowered voice.

'I think you had better explain,' she said.

Susan took a deep breath. She tried to smile but it didn't come off. 'I'm surprised you haven't heard of the happenings around here. It made a little stir in the newspapers for a time.'

'I've been rambling about Mexico, remember,' Gaye said. 'I told you that on the phone.'

'Yes, I forgot.' Susan paused again. When she began her narrative, it was as though she were relating a story she had heard once, one in which she had no personal interest. Only the drawn, furtive look about her, that seemed to grow worse as she told her story, revealed its pertinence to her.

'Some weeks ago, they found one of the local girls dead. She was in the woods, horribly mutilated, as though she had been set upon by wild animals.'

'What sort of animals?'

'There was talk of wolves.'

A cold shiver ran the length of Gaye's spine. She thought of herself in the darkened woods earlier, and that eerie wail that had frightened her so. 'I didn't think this was wolf country,' she said aloud. 'I thought, in fact, that wolves were very nearly extinct.'

'There's been a lot of argument about that,' Susan said. 'They were thought to be extinct, certainly in this part of the country. This never has really been wolf country, but those who saw the body and who are familiar with such things say it was a wolf, or wolves.'

Gaye wondered if she should mention her own experience, but she decided that Susan was already frightened enough, for whatever reason of her own. And, really, what could she say? She had heard something, but exactly what, she didn't know. She kept her silence and nodded for Susan to continue.

'Four days ago,' Susan went on, 'there was another death, just like the first one. A local girl, found mutilated in the woods. Again she looked as though she had been set on by wolves.'

'How awful,' Gaye exclaimed. 'I can certainly understand your being afraid here, but what has this to do with Walter?'

Susan got suddenly to her feet and began to pace to and fro. 'Walter knew both those girls,' she said.

'I would hardly be surprised. He's lived around here most of his life, hasn't he? And if they were local girls, why then . . . '

'Walter is an incorrigible snob. You surely don't think he hobnobbed with every common person in the town.'

'No,' Gaye said, surprised by Susan's vehemence, 'but that doesn't mean he couldn't know them.'

'Oh, Gaye, must you always be so damnably innocent?' Susan's eyes flashed with annoyance. 'Don't you understand what I'm trying to tell you? Both those girls were old flames of Walter's. He'd flirted with both of them, gone with them, made them both all sorts of promises, including vague hints of marriage.'

'How do you know this?'

Susan laughed bitterly. It made her look very old and cynical. 'Do you think I've lived here all this time without going through all his personal papers? There are photographs, gushing love letters, the works.'

Gaye thought for a moment, trying to fit together the pieces of information Susan had given her. 'Still and all,' she said, 'I don't see how that makes Walter a murderer. He couldn't just be doing away with every girl he ever flirted with, or I would know about it, don't you think?'

She hadn't meant it to sound sarcastic, but Susan took it that way. 'Oh, I know, I know, I treated you shamefully, so did he, but I've had time enough to regret it, I assure you. Do you think I've been happy here? Do you think it's been worth the anguish I've suffered every time I thought of you?'

Gaye felt uncomfortably that Susan was playing a well-rehearsed scene. She wished she did not have to sit through it, but she knew from past experience that it would be useless to try to divert Susan's attention. She would say what she had planned to say. Nothing — not even if a pack of wolves were to come, snarling and slobbering, into the room from the terrace — nothing would interfere with her intentions.

'You don't know Walter,' Susan said. 'You thought you did. So did I then. We thought he was glamorous and suave and sophisticated. Oh, yes, he's all of that all right, and a lot more. He's cruel and thoughtless and selfish. I've lived here like his slave. Another beautiful ornament for the house of Cray, that's all I've been. Oh, how I've envied you. Isn't that a laugh, to discover that all these years I've envied you, your freedom, your happiness?'

She came to a long pause, wringing her hands before her. Gaye knew that she was

43

expected to say something. The truth was, she was moved despite herself, because for all Susan's play-acting, she had not the slightest doubt that what Susan said was true. Undoubtedly Walter was all those things; she had come to realize it herself in the years she'd had to contemplate him. Of course, Susan was thoughtless and selfish herself, but harmlessly so, at least. She was not intentionally cruel and her greed was an unthinking kind.

'I'm sorry you've been unhappy,' Gaye said aloud, and meant it.

'Gaye, darling.' Susan came to her quickly, dropping on her knees so that she could embrace Gaye. 'I've been hateful, I know that. And I made up my mind that I wouldn't pain you any more. I had gotten myself into this awful place and I would endure it on my own. I would have kept that promise, too, if only I weren't so frightened.'

Of that, there could be no doubt. Susan looked up into Gaye's face, and it was evident that she really was frightened. The fear could be seen lurking in her plentiful tears.

'Walter did say he would kill me before he would permit me to leave. At first, I thought he didn't mean it, but then I thought about those girls, and I looked through his things again and found out that their letters were practically the same, declaring their love for him, insisting that he keep his promises to marry them, and I became genuinely terrified.'

'But that could be coincidence,' Gay said. 'Why would Walter want to kill them, simply because he once exchanged love letters with them?'

'I don't know,' Susan fairly wailed, getting to her feet again to resume her pacing. 'There's something else, though, that I haven't told you, that I haven't told anybody. After the last one was found . . . dead, I discovered something. I had gone down to the kitchen late one night. I was hungry and I wanted a glass of milk. I was surprised to find a fire in the stove.'

She paused and actually managed a smile. 'We have a modern range, of course, but that silly Cajun woman won't cook on anything but an old cast-iron monstrosity from the Middle Ages. Anyway, there was a fire going in it, but it was the middle of the night. I was puzzled, so I opened it and looked in. There was a shirt inside, or rather, the remnants of a shirt. Everything was burned up except part of a sleeve and the cuff. Gaye, it was Walter's shirt — and it was drenched with blood.'

'I see.' Gaye did not know what more to say. It was so difficult to imagine Walter doing anything violent. He was so calm and shrewd. Violence seemed more likely of his hot-tempered brother.

When that thought occurred to her, she asked, 'Was Carlton here then?'

'Carlton?' Susan dismissed him with a derisive sneer and a wave of her hand. 'Yes, he was here, but you needn't worry about him. He's too big a fool to do anything like that, and anyway, he's never in his life thought of anything beyond his immediate pleasure. Anyway, it was Walter's shirt, no mistake about that. It was one I had bought him.'

'Did you keep the shirt?'

Susan shook her head. 'No. I suppose

you'll think I'm foolish, but I let it burn. I couldn't very well have kept it, don't you see? If Walter had found it in my possession, he'd have guessed at once what I suspected.'

Gaye stood and put a hand on Susan's shoulder. 'It's all still too murky for me to see anything clearly, but if you're really frightened here, then we certainly ought to go away, at least for a while. Perhaps after a month in Los Angeles, you will look at it all differently.'

'No, I won't, I know I won't. You think I'm being hysterical, but I know what I see and feel, and I know it's dangerous here. That's why I wanted you to come, so you could help me get away.'

'If you think it would do any good, I'll talk to Walter,' Gaye said. 'Not about the deaths or anything like that, just about your coming to stay with me for a while.'

'No, you mustn't do that!' Susan went positively white with terror, and she gripped both of Gaye's hands in her own fierce grip. 'You don't know how angry he'd be. There's no telling what he might say or do.'

Susan's fear was contagious, and when a board somewhere nearby creaked, as they will do in old houses, Gaye had to restrain herself from looking over her shoulder, but she still thought Susan was being a little hysterical. She knew, too, that it would be wise for her to remain calm. To admit that she too was afraid would be to encourage Susan's fear.

'What do you think we should do, then?' she asked.

The matter-of-fact tone of her question, and her obvious willingness to help, seemed to relieve Susan a little. 'For a day or two, nothing,' she said. 'I've thought it all out. If we tried to leave right off, just when you've gotten here, Walter would be suspicious, but in few days' time, I thought you and I could plan a little trip somewhere — nothing too far or too fabulous, but there are some lovely views around here and no one would think a thing if we packed a picnic lunch and went out for a drive one day.'

'And we'd just keep on driving, is that the idea?'

'Yes. We could be in Los Angeles before

Walter ever dreamed we were leaving for good.'

Gaye thought immediately of several flaws to that plan. For one thing, they could hardly take their luggage along on a picnic, without raising certain suspicions. Far more to the point, if Walter really did not want Susan to go, and was willing to resort to violence, there was every reason to suppose he would follow them to Los Angeles. With her address and phone number in the book, he would not have any great difficulty in finding them.

She thought, however, that perhaps this was not the time to bring these questions up. Susan looked calmer and happier than she had all evening, and Gaye decided it might be better to let well enough alone for the moment. Later, in the light of day, they could discuss this further, but night and the gloomy shadows that hovered in the corners of the room encouraged one to fearful thoughts.

'All right,' she agreed, patting Susan's hand. 'Don't let it worry you anymore. We'll bide our time for a few days and then be on our way. In the meantime, we could both use some rest. I've been driving all day, and you look like you haven't slept in a week.'

Susan smiled with genuine affection. For a moment she looked like the Susan of old. Gaye felt a tug at her heart. What had they done to her sister, these years here with Walter in this dreary old place?

'I'm so glad you came,' Susan said. 'I knew that I could count on you, no matter what was in the past.' She gave a quick look around the room. 'I hope you'll be comfortable here. It's the pleasantest room in the place. Is there anything you want? I could have Louise bring some hot cocoa.'

The transition from frightened sister to thoughtful hostess was so abrupt it would have been incongruous in anyone but Susan. 'No, I'm all right, thanks,' Gaye insisted.

At the door Susan kissed her good night and slipped quietly from the room. Gaye turned from the door and then, feeling a little silly, turned back and carefully slid the bolt into place.

Her bag had been brought already, and her things neatly put away. She undressed leisurely and slipped into a cool, sheer nightgown, but in the dark, the room seemed close. She got out of bed, cautiously maneuvering the little step stool at its side, and went to the doors to the terrace. She opened one set of shutters to let the night air in, although she left the door closed. Outside, the moon illuminated the terrace unevenly.

She stared at the darkness of the wood, so very near. She had meant to ask Susan where those two unfortunate girls had been found, but the question had slipped her mind. She shuddered again when she thought of her own foolish venture into the woods. Her thoughts went to the man she had seemingly hit. So much had happened since to occupy her thoughts, that she had almost forgotten him, callous though that sounded. Who could he have been, she wondered now? Why had he run like that, rather than let her help him?

An ominous thought crossed her mind. What if Susan were half-right, what if those girls had been the victims, not of a wild beast, but a murderer, and suppose the murderer were someone other than Walter, which was almost certainly the case, Susan's fears notwithstanding.

The man who had darted in front of her car and then disappeared into the forest might have been that murderer. Perhaps he had even run into the forest to lure her into its darkness.

'Oh, stop it,' she told herself, managing a giggle — which was, nevertheless, a trifle nervous. 'Next I'll envision him howling at the moon while he made a supper of one of my limbs.'

It was the house, she thought. Isolated, dark, musty, it would tend to inspire gruesome thoughts of death and dark deeds. And then, Susan's fear — that had been real enough, but that did not make it well founded. She could easily imagine Walter making some rash statement in the heat of a quarrel, and of course a man would try to keep his wife from leaving him, especially if the wife were as beautiful as Susan, and the man aging rapidly and losing his looks.

Susan had always tended to dramatize

and exaggerate. The fact that he knew the two dead girls meant nothing. That was a coincidence — and not even a very striking one. From what she gathered, there was not even any reason to think that the girls were murdered. The prevailing opinion seemed to be that they had been set upon by a beast of some kind.

She thought of the shirt Susan had found burning, and frowned. That was a little strange, but often the most innocent acts, when filtered through an active imagination, looked ominous. Walter had lived his life near these woods. More than likely he was a hunting man. The blood could have come from a hunting accident. Blood looked like blood, and there was nothing to say that what Susan had seen — or thought she saw — was really human blood.

'No, there's nothing at all to it,' she concluded, going back to bed. She would go along with Susan's schemes and if Susan still wanted to go in a few days, then they would somehow manage to go, if only into San Francisco for a mini-vacation. She would talk to Walter discreetly, make him understand that even the most devoted wife sometimes needs to get away.

It was ironic that she should be put in the position of patching things up for Susan and Walter, but she was glad that she could, and glad that she had come to Craywood, because she had finally put all those ghosts to rest.

For no particular reason, she thought of Carlton Cray. Now there was someone really frightening, if in an altogether different way. If ever a man was born to excite a woman's romantic hopes, it was he. And, she added grimly, born to dash them as well. He was like a wild animal himself, exciting and dangerous.

That thought made her frown. It was an unfortunate simile under the circumstances. She turned on her side and declared her intention to go to sleep.

Tired though she was, sleep eluded her. She found herself watching the play of light and shadow on the ceiling. A groaning as the house settled itself in for the night brought her to a sitting position in the bed. She laughed at herself and tried her other side.

The house was unpleasant. Just being here was uncomfortable. She wished she did not have to stay. It occurred to her that perhaps a room on the ground floor was not completely safe. She wondered how sturdy the shuttered doors were. If a beast from the woods — say, a bear — came up to them, would they hold him out?

She nearly got up to check them and then held herself back. It was not that her uneasiness left her, but rather the knowledge that, if the doors proved to be flimsy, she would feel worse than ever. As though to prove that the subject had ceased to trouble her, she turned her back to them.

She could still see, however, the pattern of moonlight and half-open shutters on the opposite wall. She stared at it for a long time. Her eyelids grew heavy. At one point she thought a shadow marred the regularity of the pattern and her eyes flew open, but she realized at once that her eyes had indeed had to fly open, and if they had been closed, then the shadow could only have been her imagination.

But were those noises only her imagination? She lay for a long time before she comprehended that she had truly been asleep — not just dozing, but actually asleep.

Had the noises been a part of sleeping, or waking up? She squeezed her eyes shut hard and opened them again, trying to clear her thoughts. What exactly had she heard? A shuffling sound, a faint scratching, as of someone trying to gain entrance, or . . . something. A rattling of the doors, or was that only her troubled dreams haunting her?

She could still see the shadows on the far wall. They were fainter but still distinct. Anyone standing beyond them would have been silhouetted by the moonlight.

Only, she thought, and her skin felt creepy despite her best efforts, she had only opened the top bank of shutters. The bottom section of the doors, where the shutters were closed, stood four, maybe four and a half feet from the floor. If there were an animal outside, a bear or a wolf, it would throw no shadow on her wall.

She strained her ears, listening. She could hear the sighing of the wind in the trees beyond the terrace. 'I must have dreamed it,' she thought. She gave her pillow a hearty thump and made as though to go back to sleep.

She could not fool herself, though. She would never go back to sleep until she had gone to the shutters and looked out, and assured herself that there was nothing at all there.

After a long several minutes, she sighed and got up from the bed, again clambering down the small stepstool. She went quickly and silently across the room, to the shutters, and stretched to look down.

Of course there was no slobbering wolf waiting to spring. She almost laughed aloud, although the laugh lingering in her throat had been more than ready to change its mind and come out a scream if need be.

Her eyes made quick sweep of the terrace and the dark line of the woods.

Laughs and screams alike caught in her throat. There *was* something there. No beast this, but a man, unless wolves had taken to smoking cigarettes.

When he inhaled, the brighter glow was sufficient to let her see Carlton Cray's face. In almost the same moment he tossed the cigarette aside and stepped back, into the darkness of the wood, and disappeared from sight. She stared after him, but she could see nothing. She might almost have dreamed his presence there, along with the mysterious noises at her door.

Or had she dreamed them? Carlton had been there, just beyond her terrace. Nor had he been passing idly by, on some reasonable errand. He had been standing quite still, and he had been staring quite hard at her shuttered doors.

4

Although she waited for what seemed hours, there was no further sight of Carlton. At last she realized that her legs were nearly numb from stretching to see in all directions. She returned uneasily to her bed. Staring up at the ceiling, she tried to imagine what Carlton's moonlight watch could mean. Had he tried the door to her room? Those furtive sounds lingered on the border of certainty. She thought they had been real, but she could not say absolutely.

She fell asleep with the question churning about in her mind. It was still there when she awakened. She got up at once and went to the shuttered doors, throwing them open onto the terrace.

It was a lovely morning, the sun bright and golden, the sky above blue and crystalline. Gaye breathed deeply of the pine-scented air. For a moment it seemed that everything must surely, Pippa, be right with the world. The fears and questions of the night seemed no more than an unpleasant dream.

She frowned; but they had not been altogether a dream. It had been real, at least part of it had. She stepped out onto the terrace and walked toward the trees bordering it. How innocent and inviting the woods seemed now. A blue jay scolded somewhere nearby.

Between the edge of the terrace and the forest itself, the grass had withered or been worn away, and the dirt was a loose layer of dust. She looked at it, thinking how unfortunate it must be in the rainy season — and there, in the dirt, was a cigarette butt, surely the same cigarette she had seen Carlton toss aside the night before.

Something else caught her eye, too, as she stared down — marks in the unpacked dirt. She went toward them. At first she had thought they were footprints, but as she got closer, she saw that they were not.

What were they, though? They appeared to be tracks of some sort, and they were staggered as though left by a walking creature, but she had never seen anything like them. Certainly they could not have been left by a wolf or a bear or any of the other beasts of the forest she had imagined during the night. They were more like hoof prints, the sort of mark a horse might leave, but they were too small for any horse she had ever seen, and they were paired, as if the horse had walked on his hind legs only, in a staggered line.

There was only a brief trail of the prints. She realized with a shudder that they led from the terrace into the forest. If she could have made them out on the flagstone, would they lead from her door? It was impossible for her to tell, but of one thing she felt certain: something had been on the terrace during the night. In the loose dirt, the tracks would surely not have remained more than one night.

She thought again of Carlton, standing near here, but no, these were assuredly not human prints, whatever they might be. She did not let her thoughts stroll too far along that path.

'Well, what a charming sight with

which to greet the morning,' a voice said from behind her.

She knew immediately that the voice was Carlton's. She turned quickly, to find him standing at the corner of the house, smiling warmly.

'Good morning,' she said, blushing as she remembered she was in her night-dress.

'Good morning. Have you lost something?' he asked.

She realized she had been staring at the ground when he found her, but something held her back from telling him the truth. She had a sense of guilt, as though he had caught her in something improper.

'No,' she said, starting back toward her bedroom. 'I was just getting some morning air.'

'Breakfast is on,' he called after her.

She went in and swung the door closed without answering, but she could not resist the temptation to take a cautious peek through the shutters. She saw Carlton cross the terrace with only a single quick glance in her direction, but the shutters concealed her. He went directly to where she had been standing. His eyes were down now, too and she recognized the moment he saw the tracks in the dirt. While she watched, he studied them for a moment, even stooping down to look at them more closely. Then he stood again, but before he left he erased the tracks with his feet.

She was disappointed. She would have liked an opportunity to try to identify those marks in the dirt, but she had seen them, and she would know them when she saw them again. He could not erase that fact. At least, she thought with a chill as she turned from the shutters, he could not very easily do so.

★ ★ ★

She saw Carlton again when she came into the dining room. He was just finishing a roll and he stood when she came in. She had intended to be cool with him, but she found herself returning his warm smile despite her intentions. It would be difficult, she thought, to remain cross or distant with Carlton, at least if he had set out to charm you — and apparently he had set out to charm her.

'Good morning again,' he greeted her. 'In case no one told you, breakfast is a highly informal occasion here. To put it in the simplest possible terms, everyone helps him or her self.'

He indicated the buffet on which had been set fruit, rolls, pitchers of fresh cream and urns of coffee, as well as the necessary china and implements.

'It looks quite sumptuous,' she admitted. 'But I'm afraid I'm one of those coffee-only types.'

'Let me,' he said, coming at once to the urn and pouring her a cup of the steaming brew. 'Cream, sugar?'

'Neither, thank you.' She took the cup and let him help her with her chair. She smiled in amusement. Whatever the purpose of his night-time vigil, it had certainly improved his manners.

She remembered hers, then. 'I'm afraid I must apologize for my rude remarks last evening,' she said, looking up at him. 'And also thank you for not repeating them to the others.'

'I think it is I who should apologize,' he said, smiling down at her. 'After all, I goaded you into making those comments, when I ought to have told you right off who I was.' He sounded quite sincere.

'Then let's both forgive and forget,' she said. She was thinking again how handsome he was. When he smiled at her, with those blue eyes of his sparkling, it did seem that her heart beat a little faster.

Easy, girl, she warned herself. *If ever a man was not meant to be true, this is the one. And you've already suffered one broken heart at the hands of a Cray.*

Fortunately for her sense of balance, the mood was shattered as Susan came crashing into the room from the kitchen — crashing, because she let the door slam back hard against the wall.

'Damn,' she said, looking flushed with anger. 'Good morning, Gaye. Hello, Carlton.' She poured herself a cup of coffee.

'I must say, you make your morning greetings dramatic,' Carlton remarked.

Susan ignored him and sat down opposite Gaye. 'You don't know what it can be like,' she said with a sigh, 'running a place like this. If it isn't one thing it's another.'

'What is it this time?' Gaye asked.

'The servants.' Susan's inflection reduced that working class to the lowest level of humanity.

'The Stoddards?' Carlton asked. 'Surely they haven't quit. Why, they've been here forever.'

'No, they haven't quit, but they might as well have. They refuse to stay here, they say they'll only come and work during the days, but they positively have to leave before sundown.'

'That doesn't sound too awful,' Carlton said.

'Doesn't sound too awful?' Susan was incredulous, and angrier than before. 'We'll be eating dinner in the middle of the afternoon, that's all.'

'Or preparing it ourselves,' Gaye said quietly. 'You were always an excellent cook in the past.'

Carlton had a scornful expression on his face. 'That was before she became a wealthy Cray,' he said in a tone to match his look.

Susan shot him a frosty glance and would have replied, but Louise came in just then to refill the coffee urn. She wore a sullen expression that suggested the subject had already been discussed at some length in the kitchen, and not happily.

'Oh, Louise,' Susan said, apparently still not satisfied that things had been settled, 'you've simply got to reconsider. If you're afraid of going home in the dark with those deaths that have happened, then we'll arrange to drive you home at night. Carlton will take you, won't you Carlton?'

She turned plaintively toward Carlton as she said this. As a result, she did not see Louise's reaction to the suggestion, but Gaye was watching the servant and was astonished at what she saw. The idea of having Carlton drive her home not only did not reduce Louise's fears, but it added to them considerably. Her eyes went wide and she turned pale.

She recovered herself quickly, and turned her back so that her emotions should not be apparent. 'We go by sundown,' she said, busy pouring the coffee, and added, emphatically, 'before sundown.'

Gaye glanced quickly in Carlton's direction. Had he seen the old woman's fright? It was impossible to tell. His face, that had been warm toward her a few minutes before, had become an impassive mask.

Louise went out before Susan could think of any further argument. Carlton drained his cup and set it aside.

'If you will excuse me,' he said, 'I'll see about your car, Miss Hanson.'

'You could have helped with Louise,' Susan said as he went toward the hall.

'When two women are quarrelling, a wise man maintains his silence,' he said, and went on out of the room.

'A wise man,' Susan repeated with derision. 'He hasn't the sense he was born with.'

'I don't understand why you two are so bitter toward one another,' Gaye said tentatively.

'He hates me,' Susan said. 'Because I'm married to Walter, and he's insanely jealous of his brother.'

'Jealous of Walter? But it seems so silly. Carlton has no reason to be jealous of anyone. He has money, good looks . . . ' She paused, thinking perhaps she had said more than she should have. Another thought crossed her mind, too — perhaps Susan was the reason for Carlton's jealousy. Men had always fallen head over heels for Susan. Why would Carlton be an exception?

'Good looks? Yes, I suppose he has,' Susan said. 'I had never thought of him as being handsome, he's too outdoorsy, high-spirited for me. But he doesn't have any money. At least, not that he's free to do with as he chooses. It's all in trust funds, his and Dennis's, and Walter controls the purse strings. Carlton gets an allowance, of course, a generous one, if you ask me, but don't think he doesn't hate having to come to Walter for every extra penny he spends.'

'Isn't that rather an unfair arrange-ment?' Gaye asked. 'After all, Carlton isn't a child. I could hardly blame him if he resented being treated like one.'

'Their father was no fool. He knew that Dennis would never be more than half a man, and that Carlton would always remain what he was, a playboy. Walter was the only one with sense enough to take care of the family fortune.'

Gaye studied the remains of her coffee thoughtfully. She wondered again if part of Carlton's resentment might have to do with Susan herself. The thought gave her an unexpected pang. It was not an unlikely prospect. Carlton was the sort of man who would appreciate a beautiful woman, any beautiful woman. Gaye had lived in the news world, which was for the most part a man's world, long enough to recognize the type. And Susan had lived here for five years. Granted, she had said that Carlton travelled, but he obviously spent part of his time here in this remote house. Surely a woman as lovely as Susan must have been a great temptation to him from time to time.

'Well, don't we look gloomy,' Walter said, coming into the room. He looked from one of them to the other.

Gaye blushed as she realized just where

her thoughts had been leading her. Worse, they had made her gloomy, too. Why should she care if Carlton were tempted by, or even madly in love with, Susan? She ignored the mocking little laugh inside her head.

For a suspected murderer, Gaye reflected, Walter was in awfully good spirits, better than anyone else on this particular morning, it seemed. He ate heartily and chatted with as much ease as he had the night before. Not even the news about the servants seemed to perturb him.

'I'll talk to them,' he assured his wife.

'How many servants are there?' Gaye asked. She had seen no one but Louise.

'Just Louise and her husband, Turkey,' Walter said.

'Turkey? Isn't that an odd name for a man?' Gaye said.

'Yes,' Walter said with a little laugh, 'But the truth is, he does look like one.'

Gaye laughed. 'I shouldn't think he'd be very flattered by that.'

'I suppose if it had come from some other source, he might have been put out by it,' Walter said. 'But it was Dennis who gave him the name when he — Dennis, that is — was just a little thing. The Stoddards virtually raised him. They dote on him, always have. Stoddard found the nickname merely amusing, and in time everyone has taken to calling him that. I think by this time most people have forgotten his real name. Mike, I think it is, but there, you see, I'm not entirely sure myself.'

He finished eating and got up for some fresh coffee. 'You ought to have Susan show you about the place today,' he said. 'It's somewhat rustic, but I think rather beautiful in its own, gothic, way.'

'I thought about going for a hike,' Gaye said. 'But I wonder how safe the woods are, after those deaths.'

The ominous rattle of Walter's cup in his saucer reminded her that she was on shaky ground. She saw the look of alarm that flashed over Susan's face, but Walter, behind her, missed it.

'How on earth did you know about that?' he asked.

'I read it in the papers. It warranted the second page in Los Angeles.' She swallowed the last of her coffee to wash down the untruth.

'How unfortunate,' Walter said, taking his seat again and looking quite as calm as before, 'that you should have had your impression of our home spoiled by adverse publicity.'

She took a stab in the dark, ignoring the warning looks she was getting from across the table. 'What was it anyway? I seem to have forgotten the details.'

'There weren't many,' Walter said, smiling down the table at her. 'The victims were apparently attacked by some wild animal, a mountain lion, perhaps, although they're rather rare.'

Gaye studied her nails intently. 'I had some sort of notion that it was something else,' she said. 'I don't know where I got the idea. Didn't the newspaper say a hoofed beast of some sort? I can't think what it could be, though.'

'I can't either,' Walter said. 'Aside from a few horses and some cows, and maybe a goat or two, there's not likely to be any hoofed animals around here, and they certainly aren't a threat to anyone — unless, of course, it was old Pan.'

'Pan?'

'The mythological god of the forest, half man, half goat, and all devil. He was also the god of fear.'

Gaye looked down the table at Walter. He was smiling. She wondered if he were teasing her. 'I think it would be more reasonable to suspect a mountain lion. Or perhaps a wolf.'

Walter's smile remained fixed. 'There are no wolves in this area,' he said simply. He turned to his wife. 'Susan, why don't you show Gaye around Craywood? If she's frightened you need go no further than the gardens.'

The two women stood up, but Gaye could not resist a parting shot. 'I'm dominated more by curiosity than by fear,' she said, looking back from the doorway. 'If I thought I were in danger from some mythological beast, I might risk letting him eat me purely for the sake of finding out exactly what kind of beast he was.'

Walter only continued to smile.

Craywood was even larger than she had imagined, three full floors and an attic above. Even in the light of day, however, Gaye found it gloomy and uninviting. Perhaps, she reasoned with herself, it was only because Susan's fear had infected her. Perhaps under some other circumstances she might have found it lovely and warm. Certainly Walter did, and Carlton . . . but she could not remember Carlton indicating any particular feelings toward Craywood. If, as Susan had said, he hated his brother, then maybe he hated Craywood, too. His frequent travels suggested that he did not in any event feel closely bound to the place.

The wing in which she had slept was the closest contact between forest and house. In front of the house a wide lawn had been luxuriantly landscaped. At the other end of the house from her bedroom there were more lawns stretching down to the wilderness that surrounded them, but the trees were further away here. In the back were gardens, with an artificial pond and some statuary that Gaye found regrettably crude, among them one that she thought might be the forest god of which Walter had spoken — lower limbs suggested a hairy goat, but one prancing on his hind legs, while his upper torso was human, except for the horns protruding from a wiry mop of hair. He played pipes and seemed to regard them with a wicked leer.

'Walter's Pan?' she asked Susan.

Susan shrugged, her thoughts on other things. 'Tomorrow,' she said, 'Or the day after, I'll suggest a picnic. Try to be pleasantly surprised.'

Gaye wondered what she should say. Susan's plan seemed no more reasonable to her now than it had the night before, but at least Susan was calmer, more in control of herself, and she hesitated to undo that. She decided to keep her reservations to herself for the present. Later in the day, she would find an opportunity to talk privately and frankly to Walter. After that, she could decide exactly what she wanted to do. If, as she supposed, he were open to her suggestion, she and Susan would leave shortly on a little holiday. On the other hand, if he proved as adamant about Susan's leaving as Susan had insisted he did, then perhaps something a bit more clandestine would be in order. She would cross that bridge when she came to it.

Susan returned shortly to the house, and Gaye stayed in the garden, grateful to have some time to herself. If Craywood were gloomy and depressing, at least the grounds were lovely — except for that leering faun.

She strolled past him, giving one of his horns an appeasing pat. A path led along a hillside bordering the woods. She followed it and rounded a bend to see before her a lovely view of a wide green valley that stretched for what must have been several miles. A rock wall supported the path, but there was a ledge just below, from which she thought the view must be especially good. The climb down was no chore and in a minute she was standing with the world at her feet, or at least a great green expanse of it. For a moment she could understand why Walter loved the place so.

She became gradually aware, though, that something had changed. Without knowing how she knew, she felt certain that she was no longer alone, and that she was being watched. She continued to look out over the broad valley, but her attention was behind her, on the path she had followed. Someone was there and had been for several minutes, she was sure of it. The silence was frightening. She waited for him to speak.

Finally she could stand the suspense no longer. She turned slowly about and looked up. Dennis Cray sat in his wheelchair on the path above her. He did not seem to mind being caught staring. Indeed, he continued to stare.

'Hello,' Gaye said finally, to break the silence.

For a moment more he said nothing. When he did speak, he ignored her greeting and said, 'That's Blessed Point.'

'Which, I suppose, is blessed with legend,' she said.

'Whoever stands there and wishes, will be blessed with true love and good fortune.'

Gaye laughed and said, 'Then you ought to join me.'

As soon as she had said it, she regretted it. She had forgotten those twisted limbs of his, which would hardly permit him to climb down over the rocks. Her dismay only seemed to amuse him, however.

'I think I shall,' he said. He looked back over his shoulder, along the path, and called, 'Turkey.'

In a moment another man appeared. Gaye could only think, as he came into view, that Walter had been right — the man's appearance did indeed suggest a turkey, with his out-of-proportion body, his long thin neck from which the flesh hung down loosely, and his large, piercing eyes. Even his walk was an unfortunate travesty of that bird's ungainly gait.

'I've been invited down to join the lovely Miss Hanson,' Dennis said. 'Help me out, will you, I don't like to disappoint such a pretty creature as she.'

Stoddard's strength and agility were surprising. With neither word nor facial expression, he gathered the young man into his arms, carefully tucking the blanket about the deformed lower limbs. He scrambled quickly and easily down the bluff and in a minute they were beside Gaye. Dennis wore a bemused expression. She had an impression that he was laughing at her.

'You must be very lonely here,' she said on an impulse. Despite his coldness, she felt genuinely sorry for the young man. His situation would probably not have been pleasant anywhere, but it seemed even less so in this remote spot, far from friends or diversions.

'What makes you say that?' he asked. He seemed neither to accept nor reject her sympathy. He spoke to her in fact condescendingly, as though she were the unfortunate one.

'If I were confined to Craywood, I think I would find it very lonely,' she said bluntly.

'I think you don't care much for our family home.'

'I don't know it as you do, of course.' It was difficult not to be sharp with him. His manner invited it, and yet she did not want to be. It was an exasperating quality that all of the Cray men seemed to share — you never ended up acting with them as you had intended.

'If you did,' he said, and his amusement turned to bitterness, 'you wouldn't like it any better.' With that, he apparently dismissed her. 'I think I shall go up now,' he said to the silent man holding him. Without another word or gesture, he was gone, borne swiftly and quietly up over the rocks to his waiting chair.

Gaye stared after him, expecting some word, but there was none. He was almost out of sight around the bend when she finally called after him, 'Good day.'

He did not reply.

5

Gaye returned to the house, her thoughts occupied with young Dennis Cray. She felt moved by this bitter young man and drawn to him, but she could not help but think that the years of isolation in this lonely place might have affected his mind. How could it not have done so? She wondered if it were possible to reach him yet, and by what means? Surely he was a bright young man and, notwithstanding his bitterness, she could see that he was not entirely lacking the charm common to the Cray men, at least when he chose to exercise it.

When young, Gaye's family had teased her for always bringing home stray dogs and cats and, as she got older, stray people as well. It was true, she was strong enough herself and capable, that she felt an immediate protective urge toward those who were not as she was. It was this quality that had permitted her to continue loving and caring for her sister after all that Susan had done to prove her ingratitude. She knew that Susan's faults were not deliberate faults, but the faults of weakness and inability.

Although Dennis Cray had been rude to her, or perhaps because of his coldness, she felt the burden of his unhappiness, and wished she could somehow be friends with him.

She encountered Carlton as she came into the spacious front hall. He greeted her in a preoccupied manner and she was past him, on the way to her room, before he called after her, asking her to wait. She paused and he came quickly to where she was standing.

'I saw you talking to Dennis,' he said. 'I suppose he was probably a little sharp with you.'

'A little.' She had meant consciously to deny the fact, but the truth had come out of its own accord. Carlton's eyes did not encourage even little fibs.

'You'll have to pardon him, it's only his way. He expects people to be repelled by him, and he tries to beat them to the punch by showing that he cares nothing for them or their opinions. But he isn't altogether nasty. Once you get through to him, he can be a very pleasant young man.'

'I would never have imagined otherwise,' she said. Her feelings were mixed. She was touched by Carlton's unexpected concern for his brother. It was especially interesting if one compared it to Walter's attitude. In all the time she had known Walter, he had never mentioned a disabled brother.

It was also disconcerting, however, again to discover that Carlton had been watching her. Had that been deliberate, or mere chance? Where had he been? In the house? Surely the point could not be seen from just any window.

Or had he been outside? That would suggest that perhaps he had been following her. She had an uncomfortable feeling, nothing more than a suspicion, that wherever she went, whatever she did, he watched.

But why? Jealousy over Susan? Perhaps he suspected that she might take Susan away. Or jealousy of Walter? He obviously knew she had once loved Walter, or at least had thought she did — but why should he care about that? It was years in the past.

Unless, as Susan had implied, his jealousy was the consuming, hating kind that knew no limits. If that were so . . . she shook her head, pushing those thoughts away.

'Well,' he said, seeming to sense her distraction. 'I wanted to thank you anyway. He doesn't receive a great deal of attention. God knows I'm not around all that much, and I don't think anybody else but the servants bother with him. He always says the Stoddards are his family.'

'Surely Walter doesn't neglect him altogether,' Gaye said. 'And I'm sure Susan would never be deliberately unkind to anyone so unfortunate.'

For a long moment he did not reply. When he did, his remarks were utterly unexpected. 'You make the world seem so beautiful,' he said in a low voice

She could only stare at him dumbly. His expression was no longer mocking or amused, as it usually was. She thought she read something quite different in his look.

But it was gone in an instant, shoved brutally aside. 'I wish it were,' he said in a gruff voice. He turned quickly and went away.

★　★　★

The day passed quietly. The library, Gaye found, was well stocked. She settled with a collection of Mister Maugham's stories and was astonished in time to discover that the few minutes she spent with the author were actually hours, and it was evening.

Dinner was early. The Stoddards were firm in their determination to leave before sundown. Susan fumed to no avail. Walter did not seem to mind. Carlton was amused, and made more than a few remarks, the purpose of which seemed to be simply to add to Susan's bad humor.

Afterward they had brandy before the fire in the den. It was a surprisingly cheerful scene and for once the frictions that existed between the various members of the household were kept below the surface. Only the absence of Dennis disturbed Gaye's tranquil mood.

'He stays to himself quite a bit,' Susan explained when Gaye mentioned that.

'The north wing of the house has been turned into an apartment for him,' Walter added. 'He has everything there he could want, and he seems to prefer spending his time there alone. The Stoddards look after him, of course. I suppose the rest of us only serve to remind him of his afflictions.'

Gaye could not resist a glance in Carlton's direction. He said nothing, but there was the slightest flutter of an eyelid that suggested, however vaguely, a wink. After a time, he rose and stretched.

'I think I'll look in on Dennis, and then turn in,' he said.

Gaye stood too. 'I wonder if your brother would mind my tagging along,' she asked.

She avoided looking at Susan or Walter. She thought she knew what she would see in their expressions. Carlton's was, as so often, unreadable.

'We sometimes play a game of chess,' he said.

'In which case I will excuse myself. Unless,' she added, 'you think I shouldn't come at all.'

'I myself would be delighted. And although he won't admit it, I think Dennis would be too.'

If Dennis were delighted to see her, he gave no sign of it. He greeted her as coldly as ever, although with formal politeness. The chessboard was set up and Gaye realized that she was indeed interrupting the game for which Dennis was waiting.

'I only wanted to say good evening,' she said to him. 'And to thank you for explaining the tradition of Blessed Point.'

Dennis' eyes went from her to Carlton. 'And has it held true for you, Miss Hanson?'

It was Carlton who rescued her from her inexplicable embarrassment. 'Miss Hanson was just saying what good fortune she had in such a pleasant day.' But the one lifted eyebrow and the tilt at the corner of his mouth said that he was enjoying her discomfort and might even know the cause of it. Gaye excused herself at the first tactful moment.

She went to the den only long enough to say good night to Walter and Susan, and then on to her own room. She did not have to peek through the shutters to see if Carlton was watching. His chess game would keep him occupied for some time. Probably because she knew this, she had no difficulty in falling asleep.

She awoke with her skin tingling, sitting up so suddenly that the room pitched sickeningly. It came again — a high, chilling wail. The howl, she thought, of a wolf.

She jumped from the bed, ignoring the stepstool, and ran to the shuttered doors, flinging them open. If she had taken time to think, she might have shown more discretion, but sleep had departed too recently. She was on the terrace, staring with wide eyes toward the woods, before she realized the danger of her impulsiveness.

Almost at once, Walter was at her side.

He seemed to have emerged from the shadows, and there was not even time to be startled by the suddenness of his appearance.

'Get inside,' he said, speaking with a sharpness she had never heard from him before. As if to emphasize his command, he seized her arm and turned her roughly about. Without protest she hurried back to her room and bolted the doors firmly after herself.

Scarcely had she slid the bolt than she heard a quick rapping at her door, the one from the hall. 'Yes?' she asked breathlessly.

'It's Susan, let me in,' came the reply.

Gaye opened the door and Susan ran into her arms, looking wan and frightened. 'Did you hear it?' she sobbed, clinging to her sister.

'Yes, what on earth was it?' Gaye had had time enough now to be frightened herself.

'A wolf, it was a wolf,' Susan sobbed, 'and it sounded like it was right here, just outside the house.'

'Nonsense,' Gaye said. She wished that

she felt as calm as her voice sounded, but she knew that she dared not show any fear. It would only send Susan off on an hysterical bout, to think that she were frightened too. 'Walter said there were no wolves around here, you were sitting right there when he said it. And he ought to know, he's lived his whole life around here.'

But, she thought, it had sounded like a wolf to her, too, and it had certainly seemed to be just outside. She shuddered to think that she had burst out of the house without a thought for danger.

She remembered then that Walter was still out there, alone so far as she knew. 'Where's Carlton?' she asked.

Susan drew back to give her an odd look. 'In his room, I suppose. How should I know that?'

Gaye disentangled herself from Susan's embrace. 'If Carlton somehow didn't hear that racket, he should be told that Walter is out there by himself, investigating,' she said sharply. 'Which room is Carlton's?'

'Oh, God, don't leave me alone,' Susan begged, clinging to her anew.

'Stop it,' Gaye said firmly, pushing Susan's hands away. 'You'll be all right here. I'll lock the door after myself. Which room?'

Her firm manner seemed to restore Susan's self-control. She took a deep breath and hugged herself. 'The second floor, take the main stairs, it's the third door on the right.'

Gaye went to her closet and got a robe. She put it around Susan's shoulders and led her to one of the overstuffed chairs. 'Wait here,' she said.

The door had a huge key in the lock. She took it and locked the door from the hall. Then, grateful that the hall lights were on, she hurried toward the front stairs.

Carlton did not answer her knock. Thinking it was no time for propriety, she tried the door and, finding it unlocked, went in. She was in a sitting room. Possibly, she thought, he had not heard her knock. The door to the adjoining room was open, the room dark. She tapped on the woodwork and called his name. There was no answer, and she stepped hesitantly into the bedroom.

Her hesitancy was quite unnecessary. She could see plainly in the light from the sitting room that he was not there. Nor, she realized, looking at the unwrinkled bed, had he been there that evening, at least not to retire.

She stood for a moment at the top of the stairs, trying to think what she should do. Carlton might have gone out for the evening. Something, be it wolf or whatever, was outside, somewhere near the house, and Walter was out there, too, alone and unarmed. Someone should be with him, at least go out to see if he were all right. Neither Susan nor Dennis could be of any use.

'Okay,' she thought, 'if I'm going out there, it will be with some sort of weapon, however crude.'

Downstairs, she went toward the kitchen. There was always something in a kitchen that could serve as a weapon. She found a big iron poker beside the coal stove. Holding it firmly in one hand, she let herself out the kitchen door.

She was at the back of the house. To

her left, the north wing separated her from the gardens and Blessed Point. To the right, the south wing contained her room and, on its opposite side, her own terrace. It was there she had seen Walter. Would he still be there? She tried to think where the howling had come from.

As she hesitated, the faint sound of voices came to her from the left, from the garden. Poker in hand, she went in that direction. She came around the corner of the house and stopped.

They were both there, Walter and Carlton. Walter was as she had seen him minutes ago, in pajamas and robe. Carlton was in the same shirt and trousers he had worn earlier in the evening, but his shirt was torn in several places, as though he had run heedlessly through the thick brush of the woods.

They had not seen her. Carlton sat on a stone bench, his head in his hands as though he were crying. Walter stood in front of him, half turned away from her.

'I shouldn't stay,' she thought, feeling suddenly deflated. She stepped back, around the corner and out of sight. She had not meant to eavesdrop and some extra sense told her that their conversation was not intended for her ears, but she could not help hearing Carlton's words, spoken in a voice filled with anguish.

'You don't know what it's like to be in the grip of a horror like this, to be controlled by it as though you had no will of your own.'

She let herself in by the kitchen door. She was so caught up in her own thoughts — so mystified by Carlton's words — that she forgot altogether to leave the poker where she had found it. She carried it with her, nor did she notice that the hall lights were out now, though she had left them on. She walked as though in a trance.

A sudden sound brought her out of it. She turned to see a whir of motion in the semi-darkness. Impulsively she raised the iron poker to defend herself.

Dennis Cray wheeled his chair into a patch of light that fell through one of the windows. His eyes went to the upraised poker.

'Well, Miss Hanson,' he said. 'You look positively lethal tonight.'

She lowered her weapon, feeling shame-faced. 'You heard the noises, I suppose,' she said.

'Wolves,' he told her.

'Wolves?' She echoed the word. Her voice sounded high and unnatural to her ears.

'Has no one told you of the wolves of Craywood? They've killed twice of late, in these very woods. And they're thirsting again for blood, that's why they cry like that.'

Again she had the impression that he was laughing at her. She thought of how foolish she must look, a silly girl rushing out with a kitchen poker to defend two healthy and husky men. Nor did Dennis ease her embarrassment with his grin. His expression said that he knew a great deal that she did not — and suddenly, she did not want to share his knowledge.

'Good night,' she said abruptly. She turned from him and hurried along the halls to her own room, wishing she could switch on the lights without showing herself to be a baby. She forgot the poker until she was back in her room.

Susan had fallen asleep, but she started awake when Gaye came in. 'It's all right,' Gaye assured her, putting the poker against the wall before Susan saw it and got frightened all over again. 'You can go back to your own room now.'

'Oh, I can't, let me stay here, please,' Susan begged, clinging to her. Nor did Gaye's assurances move her. 'Let me sleep here, just for tonight, please,' she insisted.

Finally, with a sigh, Gaye said it would be all right. 'I'll tell Walter,' she said.

She tucked Susan into bed and then once more let herself out of the room. She was more tired now than frightened. She wanted the night to be over, she wanted the light of day to dispel the gloom of her own thoughts and this dreary house.

She found Walter at the top of the stairs. He was on his way down, he explained, to look for Susan.

'She came to my room,' Gaye said, 'When that ruckus erupted. She was frightened. And she's asleep now. I think it would be best to let her sleep.' She did not mention how Susan had begged to stay.

Satisfied that she had done all that was needed of her, she turned to go down again, but Walter suddenly seized her arm and turned her to him. It was so swift and so unexpected that she was in his arms before she knew what was happening. There was light enough to see his face, and she was startled by what she saw there. It was evident that he meant to kiss her. He lowered his face toward hers.

Once again it was Carlton who intervened, a fact for which Gaye could not help feeling grateful. She had not heard him below them on the stairs, nor apparently had Walter, for his murmured, 'Excuse me,' made them both jump, and Walter let go of her.

As Carlton went by them, though, his eyes were on Gaye and they were cold with anger and reproach. She knew what he must think, and she was overcome with shame and with frustration that she could not explain to him what had happened.

He went swiftly up the stairs and disappeared down the hall in the direction of his own rooms without a backward glance, and a moment later they heard a door close none too gently.

The interruption had robbed Walter's gesture of its impetus. He looked as embarrassed as she was.

'Good night, Walter,' she said, and was gone quickly from him, hurrying down the stairs and to her own room.

6

Morning came, but the chill of the night remained. Susan, who had seemed the day before on the road to becoming her old self, was fairly trembling with fear that Gaye's arguments did nothing to lessen. Walter mumbled greetings to Gaye at breakfast and hurried away after scarcely touching his food. Carlton did not appear at all in the dining room, although Gaye lingered over coffee until an obviously impatient Louise had cleared everything else away.

At the risk of making Susan feel worse, at the first opportunity, Gaye asked a question that had bothered her since encountering Dennis the night before.

'Those two deaths you spoke of, where were the bodies found?'

'What makes you ask that?' Susan grew paler still.

'I only wondered.'

'In the woods here,' Susan said finally. 'At Craywood.'

Later in the day Gaye did encounter Carlton in the downstairs hall. The look he gave her was so cool that she had not the heart to try to explain the scene he had witnessed the night before, and would have gone by him with only a casual greeting had he not spoken to her.

'Dennis tells me you armed yourself to search the house last night.' Although his words were flippant, his expression was not. His customary smile, that ranged from mocking to melting, was altogether absent. He looked aloof, and harried.

'I'm afraid I must have looked rather foolish,' she said, 'But I had no idea what I might encounter.'

'You must be a very brave girl.'

She shook her head. 'I wouldn't have armed myself if I hadn't been frightened out of my skin.'

There was a long silence. He seemed to have said all he wanted to say to her, but there were too many questions plaguing her and she thought she was as likely to get an honest answer from Carlton as from anyone else in the household.

'Carlton,' she began, and after a pause,

went on, 'what was that last night?'

His silence was so long that when he finally said, 'I don't know,' she thought that he was lying, but she did not pursue the matter. The rapport that had seemed to exist between them was gone, and she knew full well what had destroyed it, but she could not bring herself to talk about that now with Carlton. After all, she had done no wrong for which she should apologize or need to explain.

The truth was that no wrong had been done at all. Walter had been tired and distracted, and had seized her as he had used to do, but he had come to his senses, and it had after all been nothing.

Why then, she thought, *am I so embarrassed to meet Carlton's eyes?*

Of course, she knew it was because of how the scene had looked to him. And it was no good to tell herself it shouldn't matter what he thought. It did.

'In your search last night, did you go outside?' he asked.

She knew that he meant: did you see or hear Walter and me in the garden? She avoided his eyes when she answered, 'I ran out onto the terrace, but Walter sent me back inside.' It was the truth, but hardly the whole truth.

Again the conversation stalled, and with a faint smile and a nod, she started on her way, but he stopped her with another remark.

'Miss Hanson,' he said. 'If there are future disturbances, perhaps you would be safer to stay in your room.'

She smiled and was disproportionately pleased by his concern, but when she was back in her room, it occurred to her that he might only have meant to prevent her overhearing any future nighttime conversations between himself and Walter.

The garage returned her car during the afternoon. Carlton had seen to everything, for which she was grateful. With her car in her possession again, her thoughts went back to the subject of leaving with Susan. She had meant to talk to Walter, but now she was not altogether at ease with him, and she postponed that conversation.

It was no longer simply a matter, though, of catering to Susan's fears. She herself wanted to leave Craywood. The previous night's events had unnerved her more than she cared to show. As the day lengthened and evening approached, she found herself growing nervous. Night did not come happily to Craywood.

Toward evening an unusual incident occurred. It was nearly sundown, and Louise had already gone, after preparing a dinner for them, to be served cold. Gaye and Susan were in the kitchen, looking over what had been made, when there came a tapping at the kitchen door.

'Don't answer it,' Susan said in a hiss, cowering away from the door.

'Don't be a goose,' Gaye said. 'Wolves don't usually knock.'

She opened the door to find a child outside, surely the most pitiful child Gaye had ever seen. Her dress was little more than a rag, patched and stitched together a score of times, and incredibly filthy. Its wearer was no cleaner. Her nails were literally black, her hair an unkempt and matted tangle.

Susan seemed even more frightened by the sight of their caller and her hand went to her throat in a gesture Gaye was beginning to recognize now, but Gaye could not understand. Notwithstanding her poor and dirty appearance, the girl hardly appeared to be a threat to anyone's safety.

'What do you want?' Susan demanded.

The girl spoke in a frightened but determined whisper. 'I must see Louise,' she said.

'You can't see her, she's gone for the day,' Susan snapped. She would have closed the door, but the child had intruded herself in the opening. Gaye, standing behind Susan, could not tell which of the two seemed more frightened. The girl's eyes grew wider still.

'Oh, she can't be, I've got to see her,' she pleaded. She held a paper bag in her hand, which she displayed now, apparently as evidence of the urgency of her mission. 'She said she had to have it today, and I'll be tanned for being late with it.'

'Is the package so very urgent?' Gaye asked impulsively. There was something terribly pathetic about the child's anguish.

She realized, now that she thought of it, that Louise had seemed more anxious than usual throughout the day, and especially when she was preparing to leave. Moreover, she had remained later than on the previous day, almost until twilight, as though she had indeed been expecting an important delivery.

The visitor sensed Gaye's greater sympathy, and gave her all of her attention. 'Oh, yes, Miss, it's the henbane, she's got to get it right away.'

Gaye had no idea what henbane might be and she doubted that it could really be a life and death matter, but the girl was genuinely distressed. No doubt the importance of her delivery had been overstressed, and she had dawdled on her way, as young girls are wont to do. Now, it seemed, she might be in for some trouble for not completing her delivery.

'Where does Louise live?' Gaye asked aloud.

'About three miles down the road,' Susan said. Her tone was disapproving. 'The girl could take it there, couldn't she?'

Gaye glanced at the sky outside. It was nearly night. She thought of the darkness of the woods, and of the two girls who had died in them.

'I'll take the package to Louise,' she said, holding out her hand for it. 'I'll drive it over right now.'

The girl thrust the package at her. 'Oh, thank you, Miss, I'm ever so grateful to you,' she said, smiling and backing away, her head bobbing up and down. Then, with the unexpected grace of a fawn, she turned and ran away, out of sight around the house.

'Oh, wait,' Gaye called. She had meant to suggest that she drive the child home as well, but it was too late, she was gone.

'Really, Gaye, you're the most impulsive creature I've ever heard of,' Susan said, banging the door shut. 'And to be taken in by that scraggly brat.'

'Who is she, anyway?' Gaye asked.

'She's no one I want around here, I can tell you that. I'll have to speak to Louise about this.' She clattered some utensils on a tray. 'Her mother's the local witch doctor, or whatever you want to call it.

And that stuff is nothing but some herbs and berries that she has prescribed for some ailment of Louise's. Take my word for it, there's no emergency.'

'She called it henbane,' Gaye said. 'Do you know what that is?'

Susan shook her head as if to say she did not care to know. 'Weeds, if you ask me.'

Gaye was tempted to look into the bag, but it was not, after all, hers to examine. 'Well,' she said with a sigh, 'the girl seemed to think it was important.'

Susan looked at her in astonishment. 'Why, you aren't really going to deliver that to Louise tonight, are you? It could just as well wait till morning.'

'But I did promise,' Gaye reminded her. 'And it can't take more than half an hour, there and back. Tell me how to recognize the house.'

A few minutes later, with Susan still scolding, she was on her way. Night had fallen in earnest by the time she found Louise's house, a modest cottage set back from the road in a grove of trees. At first, she thought she had come to the wrong place, the house seemed dark and lifeless, but as she came nearer she saw a glimmer of light, and finally she saw that heavy shutters had been fastened over the windows, blacking out all but a few shafts of light. The house had an uneasy look, as though awaiting a siege.

Her knock produced a flurry of activity within. Gaye heard the sounds of motion, whispered voices, and what might have been the moving of furniture. Not until she had knocked a second time did a timid voice ask who was there.

'It's Miss Hanson, from Craywood,' Gaye called through the thick, rough door. 'I've come to deliver a package to you. It came to the house after you left.'

There was another pause and more whispered discussion, then the sound of a bolt being lifted. The door opened a crack and Louise peered out. When she was satisfied that it was indeed Gaye, and that she was alone, the door opened wider. Louise's husband stood right behind her. Both wore expressions of fear and wariness.

The cottage itself was in an odd state.

Approaching the door a moment earlier, Gaye had bumped something with her foot, but in the darkness she had not seen what it was. Now, in the light that poured form the door, she could see that it was a large enamel basin holding, so far as she could judge, clear water. Beyond the Stoddards, all about the room within, she could see other containers of every sort and size, also filled with what appeared to be water.

Nor was that the only odd thing. With the opening of the door her nostrils had been assailed by the sharp and unmistakable odour of burning sulphur. She could see that the cottage was thick with the acrid smoke and she wondered how its occupants could bear the scent.

One thing was very clear. Whatever the contents of the package, or its purpose, Louise attached no small importance to it. She was surprised that Gaye had brought it, and overwhelmingly grateful.

'It was so very good of you,' she said, clutching the small parcel to her breast.

'It was nothing, really,' Gaye said, puzzled by the scene and the couple's behaviour. She was actually glad that they did not invite her in. Even where she stood the stench was unpleasant.

'You're very kind,' Louise said, her eyes studying Gaye's face intently. 'I told my husband that when you came, I said, 'She is good, she is not like the other one'.'

'You misjudge Mrs. Cray,' Gaye said quietly. 'Despite her very human faults, she is a very kind person herself.'

Louise shook her head vehemently. Susan's kinship to Gaye seemed to matter for little in her eyes. 'She's bad, that one. You should not stay at Craywood, you should go away at once, tonight, even.'

'But why? What have I to fear?'

Louise shook her head again. 'Wait,' she said. She swung the door partially closed. Behind it, Gaye heard Louise and her husband once again exchange whispered remarks. Then the door opened again.

'My husband will take you to your car,' Louise said. He had gone into the room but now he came out again, carrying a shotgun.

'But it's not necessary,' Gaye said, startled by the sight of the weapon. 'My car's only at the road.'

They paid no attention to her objections. 'Leave Craywood,' Louise said once more, and the door closed, and Gaye was left on the porch with Turkey Stoddard.

It seemed there was nothing to do but let him see her to her car and, in truth, when she had started again down the dark path, she was rather glad to have him at her side, shotgun and all. He stood alongside the road and watched until, with a wave in his direction, she had driven off.

She was nearly back to Craywood when another car passed going in the opposite direction. She had a glimpse of bright red and recognized the roar of Carlton's Ferrari. He braked as he passed her and in her mirror she saw him turn his car swiftly around and follow her. He pulled up at the house right after her.

'An escort?' she asked as he joined her at the steps.

He seemed still removed and distant. 'I started on an errand,' he said. 'But I thought after all that it could wait until morning.'

She did not believe him. She thought that, hearing she was out, he had come specifically to find her. The thought would have made her very happy but for one nagging uncertainty: she could not decide if he were watching over her, or merely watching her.

7

Walter and Susan were in the den. Gaye was surprised to see that there was a stranger with them. Walter introduced him as Sheriff Lester.

'Ben has handled the investigation of those unfortunate deaths in the area,' Walter explained.

Gaye felt a wave of anxiety. How had his investigation brought him to Craywood? 'I hope everything's been cleared up,' she said aloud.

The Sheriff shook his head gravely. 'I don't know. The more we clear things up, the more puzzling they get.'

'Ben thinks we've somehow acquired a pack of wolves in the area,' Walter said.

'I don't think, I know,' the Sheriff argued. He was a florid man, thick and red-skinned. At first glance he might have been thought unqualified for his job. There was no sense of keen intelligence at work, no quick perception.

When Gaye looked into his dark eyes, and observed the deliberateness of his mannerisms, she had the impression of a stubborn determination and single-mindedness. They were his saving graces. She rather thought that whatever this man set out to do, he would eventually do, and once he had made up his mind to a thing, there was no room at all for doubt.

'There were hairs around both bodies,' he said now, in the voice of a man who has already explained this several times over. 'The first time, we couldn't make anything of them, but after the second death, we sent them off to a laboratory in San Francisco to be identified. They told us they were wolf hairs.'

'There are no wolves around here,' Walter insisted quietly. 'Except in Alaska, there aren't any in the United States.'

'I thought that too,' Sheriff Lester said. 'I'll tell you what I thought, I thought maybe it was a pack of wild dogs. The reason I thought that was, back in the old days, in the days of the depression, dogs sometimes ran like that. There wasn't enough food to feed the animals and so folks just turned out the dogs, and they got to running in packs hunting food. Sometimes they'd attack animals as big as cows or horses, and every once in a while you heard of a man being attacked. That's what this looked like, like dogs had torn the girls apart — excuse me, ladies.'

He shook his head. 'Well, I didn't believe it when that laboratory told me that. I said they were mistaken. So, I had the hairs sent to another place. They said the same thing, they were wolf hairs.

'So,' he said, taking his hat from off the coffee table, 'I'm going around telling folks about it, and warning them not to go too far afield by themselves, particularly at night, until we've found these devils. Probably there's more than one. Never heard of wolves hunting alone.'

Gaye opened her mouth to speak. She wondered if the others had mentioned the disturbance of the previous night. Walter's eyes met hers. She looked from him to Susan and she knew instinctively that they had not told the Sheriff of the howling they had heard. She looked at Carlton. His expression was blank, but he answered her question for her.

'Thank you, Ben,' he said, shaking the Sheriff's hand. 'Appreciate your taking the trouble, but I'm afraid I have to agree with my brother. Whatever those laboratories say, I don't think there are any wolves around here. Remember, both those tragedies happened on Cray property. If there were wolves that close, we'd surely have seen or heard some evidence of them by this time. Animals leave trails.'

'Seems like you'd have seen some trace of them,' the Sheriff agreed. He did not seem inclined to argue the point. His set jaw said that he knew what he knew. What they believed was their affair. 'Well, I wanted to tell everyone around, that's all I can do until we find something. Good night now. Pleased to meet you, Miss Hanson.'

There was a strained silence when he had gone. Gaye could not restrain herself from asking, 'Why did no one tell him of that howling last night?'

'Because the man's a fool,' Walter said sharply. 'He'd have entire posses combing the grounds here, for nothing.'

'But how can it be nothing?' Gaye did not like being dismissed so lightly. 'And Dennis said it was wolves. He called them the wolves of Craywood.'

'Dennis was just trying to frighten you,' Carlton said. 'He sometimes displays a peculiar sense of humour.'

Gaye looked again at Susan. Her sister looked as white as if she had seen a ghost. For the first time, Gaye realized how fully right Susan had been, about one thing, at least — she should be gotten away from here, and quickly.

But in playing her waiting game, she had played them into a corner. After the Sheriff's warning, she could hardly carry off a ruse of going on a picnic, and she felt less and less inclined simply to speak to Walter about the matter.

She knew that Susan, in typical Susan fashion, had transferred the whole matter to her shoulders and was waiting for her to make a move. Her inclination was simply to say that she was leaving and wanted Susan to go with her. This was the twentieth century, as she had reminded Susan. What could Walter do, actually?

But even as this argument went on within her, she knew that she would not risk such a direct approach — would not, in fact, risk finding out what Walter might do.

Dinner was a subdued affair. When it was finished, Carlton excused himself and went again to see Dennis. Gaye did not suggest accompanying him. Not until he had gone did she realize that she had been hoping he would invite her.

She tried to read after dinner, but her attention would not remain with the novel she had chosen. It was difficult to be concerned with the misadventures of the heroine when in fact she herself was beset with problems of a much greater magnitude. Finally, she abandoned the book and gave herself over to contemplation of the situation.

Leaving was made considerably more difficult by the fact that they had no one in the house that she could look upon with certainty as an ally. Susan was frightened of Walter, and she herself had lost some of her faith in his basic reasonableness. Carlton, strong and handsome figure that he was, could not be

119

turned to. His own behaviour was too odd. Dennis, even if he had been friendly to her, would not have been much use.

She thought of the Stoddards. Louise had been grateful to her tonight, and warned her to leave Craywood. She thought she had gained a friend there, but Louise and her husband were employees of the Crays, and if they cared little for Walter or Carlton, and apparently actively disliked Susan, they were very much attached to Dennis. Would they help her at the risk of offending the Cray family? She doubted it, though if worse came to worst, she would have to appeal to them and take her chances.

Of course, she could simply leave. There was nothing to prevent her going, but she dismissed that thought almost at once. She could not leave Susan here. Even if there were no real danger, Susan thought that there was, and that was very nearly the same thing. In any case, Gaye was less and less certain that Susan was imagining the threat.

Craywood sat amid mountains and forests of high trees that sometimes let the light through and sometimes blocked it, and sometimes mystically altered it into a shimmering haze — but the shadows that darkened Craywood with gloom were more than those cast by hills and pines.

*   *   *

Carlton watched again that night. She slept fitfully and at last rose from her bed to open shutters and bring the fresh night air inside, and there he was, where he had been before, smoking and watching her room.

She toyed with the idea of going out to confront him boldly with her knowledge of his surveillance, but now some new fear of Carlton kept her inside. Before she had regarded him as a romantic threat. She had not thought of him as physically dangerous.

There was something hidden here, some evil that the Crays, all of the brothers, were trying to conceal from everyone else. Certainly Walter and Carlton had both lied to that Sheriff, and

121

she thought behind Dennis's mocking words lay knowledge of some insidious evil.

What had Carlton meant, anyway, when he had spoken of being in the grip of a horror, of being controlled as if he had no will of his own? What uncontrollable passion ruled him?

She returned to her bed and to an uneasy sleep. In the morning, she went at once to her terrace, but there were no prints in the dust this time. Had there been none, or had Carlton carefully obliterated them before she could see them?

Carlton came in to breakfast shortly after she had sat down. She was shocked by his appearance. He looked as if he had not slept at all. His face was haggard, his eyes bloodshot. He had cut himself shaving apparently, for a Band-aid covered a spot on his chin. Surely he had not spent the entire night outside her room?

She returned his greeting briefly and found that she could not look at him frankly. She knew that he must see her knowledge in her eyes. How she wished she were better adapted to deception.

She excused herself as early as possible, but the truth was, he had seemed almost unaware of her presence there, and only slightly conscious of her departure. However much she interested him during the long hours of the night, he clearly had something else on his mind this morning.

She learned soon enough what occupied him so thoroughly. Susan looked withdrawn when she joined Gaye later in the garden.

'Walter's gone,' she said without preamble. 'He hasn't been in all night.'

Gaye thought for a moment. 'Maybe this would be a good time for us to leave,' she said.

'And what if Walter came in while I was packing?'

'There's no need for a lot of packing,' Gaye said. 'We can pick up a few things in San Francisco, and everything else we need, I have in Los Angeles. You could even wear some of my things, we're still the same size.'

'I couldn't do that,' Susan said stubbornly. 'Walter has given me a great deal of expensive clothing and jewellery. I can't just leave all that behind.'

Gaye stared at her sister in surprise, which quickly became annoyance. One moment Susan was worried for her life, and the next she could think of nothing but clothes and jewellery. Gaye wanted to shake her, but she knew from past experience that getting angry with Susan would accomplish nothing.

'Oh, Gaye, I'm so frightened,' Susan cried suddenly, throwing her hands to her face.

'Yes, of course, you are, but . . . '

'Don't you see,' Susan interrupted her, her words tumbling in a rush after one another, 'if it's Walter who's killing these women, and he's been out all night . . . don't you see what that means?'

Her meaning became instantly clear to Gaye. Out for a night . . . out for a night of vicious killing? Gaye shook her head. Surely not Walter. For all that she had come to distrust him, she still could not believe that he was a wanton murderer. Yet at the same time, a grim fear haunted her that there would be another of those bodies. Perhaps even now, it lay still and bloodied in the woods surrounding them.

She shuddered and got up from the bench where they were sitting. 'We're being unfair to Walter,' she said. 'And we're overlooking the possibility that Walter himself might have been the victim of . . . of an accident. I think someone ought to look for him.'

Susan looked up at her with tear-streaked eyes. 'You can't call the police in,' she said.

'But if Walter's been hurt . . . ' Gaye argued.

'What if he's not hurt? What if someone has been killed during the night? We'd practically be pointing the finger at him, don't you see, by saying that he's been out all night like this?'

'But Susan, what are you saying? If Walter is innocent, then something has happened to him. And if, Heaven forbid, he really has killed someone, if that part of it is true, then we surely do want to bring the police into it, and at once.'

Susan began to cry again, once more covering her face with her hands. 'Oh, I couldn't bear it. Think of the shame it would mean for me, the wife of a vicious murderer. All I want is to get away from him, to safety. What do I care about any victims? They're dead and gone, and there's nothing can be done for them. I care about me, about my safety. Is that so wrong?'

Gaye was shocked by the outburst. Of course, Susan was distraught, she could hardly know what she was saying.

Or could she? A sob caught in Gaye's throat. Susan had changed so very much in these five years at Craywood. More and more, her life had centred about herself, her own wants and needs. Gaye had thought only of how unhappy Walter had made Susan during that time, but now she wondered what unhappiness Walter had suffered at Susan's selfish hand?

She put a hand on Susan's shoulder. 'You must pull yourself together,' she said. 'You don't know what sort of things you're saying. I'll talk to Carlton. Perhaps he knows where Walter is.'

She left Susan where she was, sitting and crying softly. As she started toward the house, though, an image of Carlton appeared before Gaye's eyes, as she had seen him at breakfast, tired and haggard, a man who had obviously spent a sleepless night.

She hesitated, undecided. Was it only coincidence? She tried to think of what else she might do. Her instinct was to call the Sheriff, but Susan's outburst had given her pause. More than that, she herself suffered a lingering sense of loyalty to Walter, although she would not let herself think of shielding him.

What then could she do? To whom could she talk? Stoddard? No, she shook her head stubbornly. That was only skirting the issue. Walter was Carlton's brother. It was to Carlton she should go, even if he already knew of the absence.

She found him in the library. Again she was struck by his harried appearance. She had come to expect those bright smiles of his, and his flashing eyes, and now that they were no longer bestowed upon her, she mourned their absence. A doubt assailed her, that perhaps she had let herself enjoy them too much.

'Walter's missing,' she said first thing. 'Susan says he's been out all night.'

Unless Carlton was a very fine actor, his surprise was genuine. Whatever the reason for his sleepless night, he had not been with Walter. He stood quickly, closing the book he had been reading.

'She's certain?' he asked. Gaye nodded.

'Wait here,' he said. He went past her and out of the room. She did not know what she ought to do, and decided to wait as he had said. He was back in a few minutes. Where he had gone, he did not say.

'This is a big house,' he said, speaking with a cool efficiency she would not have suspected of him. 'We don't want to jump to any foolish conclusions simply because Walter might have decided to sleep in one of the unused bedrooms. Things have not being going swimmingly for my brother and his wife, so that is not beyond the realm of possibility. Ask Susan to come here, and I'll get the Stoddards. I want to search the house.'

Within a few minutes they were all together. Carlton had taken charge. He divided the house and sent them on their ways. Gaye searched the north half of the second floor. In truth, she did nothing more than knock at each door and look in to see that Walter was not asleep or ill. She had little hope for the success of the search, but she granted the wisdom of it. However faint the possibility, it had to be explored.

The search proved to be fruitless. Gaye saw with alarm that when they regrouped, Carlton had strapped on a gun in a holster. She did not have to ask why.

'I'm going to look through the woods,' he explained, checking the revolver to see that it was loaded. 'The rest of you stay here, together.'

'Shouldn't we call the police?' Gaye offered.

'No,' Carlton answered her simply. He did not explain.

'Then surely Stoddard ought to go with you,' she said.

Again he shook his head. 'You get the shotgun from the cellar,' he told Stoddard, 'and come back here, and stay with them.'

With that, Carlton went out. Gaye followed him to the rear door. He strode across the lawn toward the woods, looking tall and heroic. She thought of what might lie in those woods — terror, death. Her heat missed a beat.

'Carlton,' she called after him.

He turned back. She had an impulse to run to him, to throw herself in his arms, but she restrained herself. 'Be careful, please,' was all she said.

He smiled at her. It was not the wide expansive grin that he so often displayed. This was something smaller, more intimate. 'Thank you,' he said. Then he turned again and walked away, and after a moment he had disappeared among the trees.

It was mid-afternoon before he returned. He looked completely exhausted and discouraged as well. He was alone, and he had found no trace of Walter.

'He hasn't shown up here?' he asked Gaye, who was waiting near the door for him.

'No.' When he was silent for a moment, she asked, 'What are you going to do now?'

'I suppose I'll have to call Sheriff Lester,' he said. 'We'll have to get a party together to search the woods more thoroughly.'

At his suggestion, she found Louise to tell her to prepare food for the hunters, something that could be kept warm for them. She persuaded Susan to take a tranquilizer and go to bed. After that, she could do nothing but wait.

She strolled through the house restlessly. Carlton was busy on the phone. She felt at loose ends and helpless to do anything. Finally, she went outside to the garden. The path that led to Blessed Point beckoned her and she strolled idly along it. She rounded the bend. It was like stepping into a different world. Craywood, with its shadows and fears, was gone from her sight, and she was alone with a soothing and romantic nature.

She reached the stone wall, thinking to climb down and enjoy the view, but she never got further than looking down at the point below.

Earlier, when Susan had told her Walter was out, she had imagined another death, another body lying sprawled somewhere, mutilated as the others had been — but she had never imagined this.

Walter lay on his back, and not all of the blood nor all of his wounds could conceal the look of utter horror on his countenance. His legs were twisted under him. One arm was thrown up as though with his last breath he had tried to drive away his attacker. At the very first glance, she thought the other arm must be twisted under him, but it was not. It was gone, torn violently from its socket. His clothes were in shreds, and wherever his flesh showed it had been clawed and torn. Everywhere, over his body, his clothes, over the earth and the grass about him, was blood. And all around him, those peculiar, hoof-like tracks that she had seen in the dust outside her own room.

Gaye swayed weakly. She wanted to scream, to run for the others — but for a moment she could do nothing but be helplessly, violently ill.

8

She was more grateful than ever for Carlton's calm strength. He left her in the den only long enough to see for himself that Walter was dead. Then, before even calling the police, he saw to it that she was over the shock of the discovery.

'Here, take this,' he said, giving her a strong brandy. 'Do you want to lie down?'

She shook her head. 'No, I'll be all right,' she told him. She surprised herself with her reserve of self-control. The sight of Walter's mutilated body still haunted her, but her speaking voice was nearly normal and she had stopped trembling. At worst, she felt numbed.

Carlton hesitated uncertainly. 'One of us has to tell Susan,' he said finally.

She looked up into his concerned face. She knew he was not asking her to assume the responsibility. He would do it himself if she did not feel up to the task, but she knew too that he thought it would be better if she handled it, and he was right. Strong and masterful as he suddenly was, Carlton was no diplomat, nor had he and Susan ever been friendly. No, it was up to her to break the news.

'I'll do it,' she said aloud. He was relieved by her decision.

'I'll have to call the Sheriff back,' he said. 'No sense in getting together a search party now.' At the doorway, he paused again. 'I suppose he'll want to talk to you, since you found the body. If you want, I can put him off until tomorrow. I can't imagine there's much you can tell him that I can't relate.'

She managed a wan smile. 'Thank you, but I will be all right, really. Let me know when he arrives.'

Susan was in her room. She had a lethargic, even wistful look about her. Gaye wondered if she had taken more than one of her tranquilizers, but she reminded herself, it was probably just as well. They would help cushion the shock.

As it were, the shock seemed to be less for Susan than one might have expected. She stared at her sister in silence for so long that Gaye wondered if she had understood. Finally, still a blank expression on her face, she sat down stiffly.

'So Walter's dead,' she said quietly. She thought for a moment and then added, 'I thought he was the one, but I see I was mistaken.'

Susan's quiet acceptance of her husband's death unnerved Gaye. There was something horribly chilling about it. 'Susan,' she said, almost thinking aloud, 'I'm going to talk to the Sheriff about our leaving. There'll be an investigation, of course, but I don't think it's likely you and I will be suspected. If whatever killed Walter was human, and even that seems incredible to me, it certainly could not have been a woman. I'm certain the Sheriff will let us go. If nothing else, we could stay in San Francisco, and come back as we're needed.'

Susan looked directly at her. Her eyes were dry, her manner steady. 'I can't go, though,' she said.

'Yes, I understand, the funeral, but we could . . . '

'Not the funeral, silly, the will.'

Gaye was dumbfounded. She thought surely she must have misunderstood, but she could not put into speech the questions that rose in her mind.

Susan smiled patiently, as one would to a slow-witted child. 'Don't you see, I may be a very wealthy widow?'

'Susan . . . '

Susan's smile turned as suddenly to a frown as a new idea crossed her mind. 'But I might not be,' she said, jumping to her feet. 'What if Walter excluded me from the will? What if he left everything to his brothers?'

She had begun to pace the room. Gaye could only stand and stare at her while she argued the point with herself. 'He can't exclude me from the community property, but that's hardly anything. All of this was his before our marriage. He could cheat me out of all that. Oh, the unfairness of it. All these years of unhappiness, just waiting to be mistress of Craywood, and to think that it might slip through my fingers now.'

It was like having a curtain lifted, to find that the scene beyond was entirely different from that which you had already imagined. She had thought she knew her sister, but now Gaye saw how utterly mistaken she had been. She looked back upon their past, and from her new perspective, she saw that Susan had not changed — she had only developed further along the way that had always been pointed.

Always, behind that numbing beauty and winning charm, had been a greedy, grasping spirit. She had never denied herself, never given of herself, except as much as was necessary to gain her various goals. It was no accident that Walter had fallen in love with her and jilted her less glamorous sister. Susan had arranged that and managed it as surely as though it had occurred upon the stage and she had been the director.

She had not even done it for love. That at least would have made her romantic. Throughout history women had committed every grotesque horror for the sake of love, and for that sake had been not only forgiven but idolized.

Susan had no such romance in her

favour. She had acted solely for the sake of becoming mistress of this bleak mansion, and to acquire the vast fortune that was Walter's.

Yet for all of this, Gaye could not hate her. If anything, she loved her the more for seeing the awful flaw in her makeup. Her sister became incredibly more pathetic, and she found herself actually hoping that Susan would not be disappointed in this, her dream for so long. How miserable she would be to be cheated of Walter's money.

Impulsively, she grasped Susan's hand. 'Oh, darling,' she said with an intensity of feeling. 'I do forgive you.'

Susan reacted with uncomprehending surprise. 'For what?' she asked.

Gaye did not try to explain. She had come to her bedroom to comfort Susan, but Susan was less distressed by Walter's death than she herself was. There was nothing she could do here, and she left Susan to her fantasies of Walter's fortune.

Sheriff Lester was more businesslike on this visit. Gaye saw him arrive, but he did not talk to her at once. He went with Carlton to the Point. Gaye went in search of Louise. She found the servant nearly beside herself. How much of her emotion was grief and how much fear, Gaye could not judge, but she could see that Louise was barely aware of what she was doing.

'I think, Louise,' Gaye said, 'that perhaps you ought to go home for the rest of the day. It's almost evening anyway. I'll tell Mister Cray it was my idea.'

'But there's so much to do, the people will want coffee, and there's no dinner ready.' The housekeeper brushed an impatient tear from her eye.

Gaye put a sympathetic hand on her shoulder. 'I'll take care of it, don't you worry.'

Louise let herself be persuaded, and left with many expressions of gratitude. Gaye busied herself making coffee for the Sheriff and the deputy who had accompanied him. By the time it was ready, they had come inside and the Sheriff said he wanted to talk to her.

There was little she could tell them about the discovery. She explained in the simplest terms going for a stroll, seeing Walter, and coming back to the house for Carlton.

'You touched nothing?' Carlton said. Although it was the Sheriff's investigation, Carlton seemed to be in charge. Gaye was surprised to see how quickly he had assumed the role of the master of Craywood — and as the older of the two surviving brothers, he was surely that now. At least, he was so until the will was read.

'Of course not,' Gaye said, thinking the question odd, but she added, 'except, I'm afraid I was sick. I leaned against something, a tree, I think. It took me a moment to recover my senses.'

'Yes, I saw that,' the Sheriff said. 'We have to ask certain questions, you understand,' he explained matter-of-factly. 'Tell me, did you happen to notice what time it was when you first saw Walter?'

'Yes, oddly, I looked at my watch as I started back to the house. It was twelve after three then. It couldn't have been more than a minute or two since I had first seen him.'

The Sheriff looked quizzically at her and then at Carlton. 'It was nearly four when you called us.'

'I'm afraid that's my fault,' Gaye said quickly. 'I was rather shaken. Mister Cray looked after me first.'

Even as she explained that, though, and her explanation seemed to satisfy the Sheriff, the thought crossed her mind that it did seem rather a long time. She had certainly not realized it was so long. What had they done? Carlton had poured her a brandy. No, before that, he had gone to look at Walter's body. How long had that taken?

At the time, still sick and upset, she had not been conscious of the time; but later, with the brandy, she had been much calmer. Surely it had not taken more than five minutes for Carlton to pour her a brandy and be sure she was all right. Had it taken him thirty or forty minutes to identify Walter and confirm that he was really dead — or had there been some other delay?

The Sheriff and his deputy seemed to have no further questions, but Gaye's curiosity impelled her to ask one of her own.

'Was it,' she said, hesitantly, and then went on quickly, 'was it the same as the others, those two young women?'

The men nodded. 'Exactly the same,' the Sheriff said. 'What gets me, though, is it being so close, right in sight of the house here, and no one seeing or hearing anything.'

'It isn't in sight of the house, though,' Carlton informed him. 'That path winds around through the trees and downhill. Blessed Point is hidden from view. And as for the sound, well, it looks as though he must have been attacked so suddenly that there was no time to cry out. And, of course, the rest of us were long since in bed and asleep.'

But, Carlton was not in bed asleep, Gaye thought suddenly. He had been standing on the terrace outside her room, watching and waiting for something. And this morning, he did not look as though he had slept at all. In the excitement, she had forgotten that. She had instinctively leaned on his strength and calm and had forgotten her own fears and suspicions regarding him.

They came back now in a rush. She even opened her mouth to speak, but her eyes turned to Carlton and he was staring directly at her. She saw something in his gaze that stopped her. He seemed to be silently pleading with her not to voice whatever thought had brought that surprised expression to her face. She tried to stare him down, to refuse what he was begging of her, but she could not. She lowered her eyes in defeat.

'You think of something?' the Sheriff asked, watching her.

She managed a small laugh and looked at him in an apologetic manner. 'I'm afraid I was thoughtless,' she said. 'I gave my sister a sedative and put her to bed, and it just now occurred to me that you would probably want to talk to her, too.'

The Sheriff looked disappointed. 'Well, yes, that's the usual thing.' He thought for a minute. 'I guess it can wait, though, till tomorrow. What I most wanted to know from her was, what was her husband doing out in the middle of the night like that?'

Again it was Carlton who had the

explanation ready. 'My brother was in the habit of staying up late, reading, going over the accounts, business like that.'

His tone suggested ever so subtly that an ordinary Sheriff could not imagine what tasks were involved in running an estate like Craywood. 'And it was his custom to check the grounds before he retired,' he added. 'You saw that he had his flashlight with him.'

The Sheriff shook his head. 'If people would just listen when you talk to them,' he said sadly. 'He must have been killed just a couple of hours after I warned you all about going out alone.'

The questioning seemed to be over for the time being. The two policemen made ready to go. 'At least,' Gaye said, trying to instill a note of optimism, 'you should be able to identify this mysterious beast now.'

'How's that?' the Sheriff asked.

'Why,' Gaye said, 'from the tracks.'

The Sheriff grinned a trifle forlornly and shook his head. 'Wish it was that easy, but there weren't any tracks, least, not anything you could identify for sure.'

'Oh, I see,' was all that Gaye said. She

144

walked with the men to the front door.

A dilapidated hearse was just pulling away. Carlton accompanied the two officers to their car. Gaye watched them for a moment. Then, hurrying, she went through the house, to the kitchen door, and let herself out. It was nearly dusk by now, and the air had a chill, but it was not that alone that made her shiver.

From the garden she followed the path to Blessed Point, trying not to recall the horror of her last trip along this path. At the rock wall, she stared for a long moment at the spot where Walter's body had lain. The grass was crushed flat, and there were still the splotches of blood on grass and dirt to tell the awful tale.

But there were no tracks. She steeled herself and climbed down over the rock wall, to the point itself. She walked carefully about, looking at the ground.

There had been tracks earlier, the same sideways hoof prints she had seen on the ground by her terrace, but they were gone now, obliterated in the profusion of shoeprints that remained. Of course, they could have been destroyed accidentally.

Perhaps Carlton, in the shock of seeing his brother dead, had unwittingly erased them with his own footprints and had never seen them — but there came to her mind a picture of Carlton by her terrace, carefully obliterating the tracks there.

She had been so absorbed in looking at the ground that she did not hear Carlton's approach. He was suddenly there, jumping down from the path above in one easy leap, and then he was before her. She turned startled eyes upon him and instinctively stepped backward, away from him, but with a swift movement he came to her and grabbed her in his arms.

She started to struggle, but his words stopped her. 'You almost stepped right over the edge,' he said.

She looked over her shoulder. It was true, she had stepped further than she realized. Another step or two and she might have stumbled over. A hundred yards below a cluster of boulders waited to catch her.

'I'm sorry,' she said, turning back to him. 'You frightened me, coming upon me that way.'

'Is that the only reason I frightened you?'

She could not help meeting his gaze. That silent plea was there again, but this time there was something else blended with it. It looked like disappointment.

'No,' she said honestly.

After a moment, he said, 'All I want is a little time. Will you give me that?'

There were many things she wanted to say, questions she wanted to ask, but his nearness, the feel of his strong hands on her arms, the look of his eyes, all combined to defeat her.

'Yes,' she said.

He held her for a moment more. She thought he was going to kiss her. It seemed as though his face had inched closer, and involuntarily her lips parted to meet his.

Then he was no longer holding her. He climbed up the wall and put out a hand to help her. On the path, she said, 'I sent Louise home. I'll take care of dinner.'

He only nodded in reply. She left him standing there and returned to the house, but there was one thing more that troubled her especially, and when she heard Carlton go into the library and close the door, she stopped in her work of preparing dinners and stole into the hall. With a cautious glance at the still closed library door, she hastened up the stairs.

Carlton had said that Blessed Point could not be seen from the house, but once before she had stood on that point, that time with Dennis, and afterward, Carlton had said that he had seen them. She could not put the question to rest until she had looked for herself.

From Carlton's sitting room, the windows offered a splendid view of the valley, and distant mountains, and closer, seemingly right at one's feet, was Blessed Point. If she looked carefully, she could even distinguish the larger patches of blood that still stained the ground. Surely one would have had no difficulty identifying a man lying there. Her heart beat wildly in her breast as she let herself stealthily out of his room and went back to the kitchen.

She had not seen Dennis Cray during that day. She could not help wondering how he had taken the news of his brother's death. She meant to offer him her sympathies, but she decided to do so when she brought him his dinner, which she would have to do in Louise's absence.

Oddly, she had expected to see no particular sign of grief. Dennis did not appear the sort of young man for that emotion, but he seemed after all to have taken the death rather hard. He looked haggard and drawn, years older than his actual age. His eyes were red and his self control, as rigid as ever, seemed this time to be an effort.

'I want to tell you how sorry I am,' Gaye offered. 'I'm sure you must know that Walter and I were once very close. I feel your loss very deeply.'

Grief seemed to have improved the young man's manners a little. 'You're a very good person, Miss Hanson,' he said.

She thought it an odd remark under the circumstances, but certainly he was an odd person. 'Thank you,' she said, setting out his dinner. 'I can't imagine what would make you say so.'

'Everyone says so,' he said, watching her.

There was such sarcasm in his voice that, forgetting his bereavement, she snapped back at him, 'And you don't agree, I gather.'

But again he softened toward her. 'I didn't at first,' he said.

She could think of nothing more to say, and gave her attention to his food. 'I hope you enjoy dinner,' she said, preparing to leave. 'I'll come for those things later.'

'You should leave Craywood, Miss Hanson,' he said as she reached the door. 'This is no place for a good person like you.'

She thought that she had never had so many people wanting her to leave a place. 'At the present I have to stay at my sister's side,' she said.

An ugly expression flitted across his face. He seemed about to make some remark about Susan, and Gaye needed no special insight to know that it would not be pleasant. He checked himself, however, and said instead, 'You should go, now, this very night.'

'Thank you for your concern,' she said. 'But I'm afraid that won't be possible.'

She went out, closing the door softly after herself. Like her own rooms, Dennis's were on the first floor, in the opposite wing. She hurried down the hall, her thoughts stumbling over one another.

She had realized, glancing with no particular intent toward his windows, that one could also see Blessed Point from Dennis's room. What had he seen that had suddenly made him fearful of her safety? What did he know that she did not know? His remarks had been no innocent advice. He had warned her, pointedly, to leave Craywood. From the moment of her arrival — no, even sooner, from the moment of that odd incident on the road — danger had hovered in the woods beyond. It had crept to the very lawns of Craywood. Now, suddenly, she had a sense that it was no longer beyond, but right within Craywood, with her in this gloomy house.

She had lied to protect Carlton. They had been lies of omission, but lies nonetheless for that. At first, she had told herself she did it to give him the opportunity to prove himself innocent, but that was deluding herself. She no longer believed him innocent. Whatever evil lurked within these walls, he was at least a part of it.

Then, she thought, hesitating at the door to the dining room, *if I did not believe him innocent, why did I lie for him?*

But she knew the answer to that question, even though she tried to hide it from herself. She had lied for him because she was in love with him.

9

Gaye was an excellent cook, and she had taken special pains with this meal because of the day's tragic events: *Consommé Bellevue*, chicken breasts in wine, a *gratin* of vegetables, and baked apples for dessert.

Despite the excellence of the food, the dinner was a dismal event. Carlton looked so preoccupied and miserable that, had she not known of his sleepless night, she would have thought him consumed with grief. She herself, torn between her love for him and her fear of him, talked in monosyllables when she talked at all. The empty place at which Walter usually sat seemed to mock them grimly.

Susan had withdrawn into herself. She ate in silence, occupied with her thoughts. Gaye dared not ask what those thoughts were. She suspected it was only a matter of time before those two strong personalities, Carlton's and Susan's, clashed.

They did so before the evening was over. At the conclusion of the meal, Carlton seemed to make an effort to take himself in hand. He addressed Susan politely, although coolly.

'I took it upon myself to begin the funeral arrangements,' he said. 'If you feel up to it, I'll discuss them with you in the den.'

She gave him a look of utter contempt. 'I'll leave them in your hands, thank you,' she said. 'I'm certain you can manage them quite as well without my assistance.'

'Very well.' He smiled acidly. 'I suppose you will want to be included in the settling of the estate?'

Susan's eyes flashed anger. 'Carlton,' she said, 'we may as well be blunt with one another. Because you were Walter's brother, I made every effort in the past to tolerate your insolence, but all that is changed now. As Walter's widow, I am mistress of Craywood, and I am certain that when the will is read you will find that it belongs to me. So you might as well get used to that idea as quickly as possible.'

Carlton continued to smile, but there was no warmth in the expression. 'I'm afraid that is quite impossible,' he said. 'Even if Walter had been so foolish, there is no way he could have left Craywood entirely in your hands. Although he was given control of the monies during his lifetime, the estate did not belong to him entirely. Only a third of it did, in case you have forgotten, or perhaps he neglected to inform you of that. The rest, including two thirds of the Craywood fortune, belongs to Dennis and myself. At the very most, you have inherited a third of Craywood, and whatever of his personal property and income Walter chose to leave you.'

Although she was obviously seething inwardly, Susan managed to keep her voice level. 'Then at the very least, if I can't depose you, you can't depose me, either, my darling brother-in-law. It would seem to be a standoff, would it not?'

For an answer, Carlton merely nodded to her. He turned briefly to Gaye. 'Good night,' he said, 'thank you for a superb dinner.'

'And Carlton,' Susan added, not to be put off, 'if I can't own Craywood, at least I can continue to live here in comfort as long as I wish. If I can't have it, then you and Dennis will certainly have me, for as long as I live.'

Gaye shivered at the ominous ring of those words. Could Susan be calling down upon herself the same, tragic fate that had taken her husband?

Fate, however, seemed contented that, for a few days at least, she had wreaked enough havoc on Craywood. The next few days passed, if not happily, at least smoothly.

Gaye paid yet another visit to Dennis, not from any sense of affection but simply because she thought it her duty to Walter's memory. If the young man was happy to see her, or grateful, he gave no sign of it, nor did he again warn her to leave Craywood. He was, in fact, quite his old self. Only once did he show any great emotion, and that was when, unthinkingly, she brought Susan's name into the conversation.

'She's a fool,' he said sharply, 'to think

she'll ever run Craywood. My brother would see that didn't happen.'

Gaye could not tell whether he meant Walter or Carlton, nor did she bring herself to ask.

Carlton and Susan seemed to have recognized their impasse and accepted it temporarily. They could hardly be described as friendly to one another, but there were no more outbursts. At dinner, they addressed their few remarks directly to Gaye, ignoring one another as fully as possible.

Gaye tried once or twice to discuss matters with Susan, but Susan seemed to have drawn a veil about herself. She was only slightly less distant with Gaye than she was with Carlton, although there was no animosity in her aloofness with her sister. Rather, it was as though Gaye had fulfilled her purpose here and was no longer of any particular importance.

Unhappily, Gaye thought it might be exactly that. Susan had called on her and tried to renew their old ties because she had been afraid and felt herself alone and friendless. Now she apparently felt that the situation was in her hands and so she need play that part with Gaye no further.

The irony, as Gaye saw it, was that she was perhaps in more real danger now than before. Previously, Susan had been afraid of Walter. Now that Walter was dead, she seemed to feel herself out of danger. It was as though the thought never entered her mind that Walter might have been murdered, but Gaye could not suggest this possibility without explaining everything that she knew, and she was quite certain that if Susan had in her possession knowledge that could harm Carlton, she would not hesitate for a moment to use it.

The Sheriff came again to speak to Susan. From Louise, Gaye learned that a search party had been organised and had combed the woods of Craywood and the neighbouring properties, to no avail. The beast or beasts that had killed three people seemed, as in the past, to have disappeared into the night air.

With Louise, as with the others in the house, Gaye had the impression that something was being held back, kept from her, but whenever she began to ask questions, Louise grew morose and silent. She had taken an apparent liking to Gaye and was ordinarily warm and friendly with her, but that friendship was not enough to induce her to talk of Craywood or the tragedies that had occurred.

Walter's funeral was held four days later. Gaye rose to find a grey rain falling. It continued steadily through the morning and was neither better nor worse when they finally prepared to go to the funeral chapel.

It was an intimate service. Susan, Carlton, Dennis, the Stoddards and Gaye herself were the only mourners at the chapel. Afterward, at the cemetery, there was a small turnout of local people. Gaye wondered how many of them were there purely out of morbid curiosity. Despite an elemental sympathy, people did seem to take some satisfaction out of the tragedies of others.

Standing next to her sister, Gaye was painfully aware of Susan's lack of grief. She held back her own tears and wondered that Susan had none. Gaye stole frequent glances at Carlton, but that handsome face was so devoid of any expression that it might have been a mask of wax.

Dennis surprised her, though. She watched as Stoddard helped him into the family's big Cadillac sedan. He was as pale as death, and both at the chapel and at the cemetery, he cried quietly but steadily into his hands. Gaye wanted to go to him and console him, but she thought he might resent her intrusion upon his grief. She wondered that Carlton was not moved to go to him but Carlton seemed not even to notice his brother's gentle sobbing.

Gaye was relieved to be in the Cadillac, finally on her way back to Craywood. It was not until they were actually there, and she was in her room, that she learned there was still another gathering before them.

'The attorney is here,' Susan said, coming unannounced into her room. 'You might as well sit in on this. It ought to be interesting.'

'Attorney?'

Susan winked mischievously. 'The reading of the will. Did I forget to tell you? Today the war is over.'

Or begun, Gaye was tempted to say. Instead, she said, 'There's really no reason for me to be present.'

'But I want you there,' Susan said. As though that settled it, she went out.

Gaye's first thought was that Susan wanted someone there to witness the triumph she seemed confident would be hers, but on a moment's reflection, she thought perhaps Susan was bluffing. Perhaps she was not really so confident as she acted. She might very well want Gaye there to help her over any defeat. With that thought, Gaye decided she should go.

Neither Carlton nor Dennis seemed to find anything odd in her joining them. The lawyer, a Mister Smith, was already in the library with them, as were the Stoddards, sitting off to themselves in one corner and looking uncomfortable. Susan came in a few minutes after Gaye.

'Well,' the attorney said, clearing his throat as Susan sat down. 'Shall we get on with it?'

There was a great deal of legal jargon that Gaye did not fully understand, but as the reading went on, she began to grow uneasy. Walter had made modest provisions for the Stoddards, but that was to have been expected, and Gaye was glad that he had done so.

Of the community property, it sounded to her as if Walter had left Susan the legal minimum. Even if he had left it all, it would not have been a great amount. Most of Walter's money was Cray money that he had inherited. He had acquired very little on his own, at least in the five years he had been married to Susan.

When it came to the Cray estate, he was even less generous with his wife. He had decreed that a certain amount of his portion of the monies involved should be set aside in a trust for her. It was not a great amount. A woman certainly could live off of it, but for a woman of Susan's extravagance it would surely be parsimonious.

He had stipulated too that she should be permitted to live at Craywood as long as she wished, but it was plain that she would live there as a guest, not as mistress of the house. For the rest, he left everything to Carlton and Dennis. Walter had, as far as he was able, disinherited his wife.

Susan's look of scorn had changed gradually into one of cold, silent fury. Gaye had ceased to watch the little man reading the will and instead had watched her sister. She was genuinely frightened by the anger she saw in Susan's expression. She feared the moment when it would erupt.

The attorney finished. Carlton thanked him and the man began to return his papers to his briefcase.

'He can't do this,' Susan said in a low voice. 'I'll fight it in every court in the land.'

Mister Smith seemed to have anticipated her remarks. 'I'm afraid there is very little you could do,' he said. 'As your husband's attorney, I must explain that he remained fully within the dictates of the law. Craywood and the Cray estates and monies were acquired before your marriage and consequently are not affected by community property laws. In any event, they are by and large set up in trusts that I think you would find inviolate. You have no claims upon them except what he has given you of his personal shares, in trust, and in permission to live on here if you wish. I can advise you in all sincerity that any money you spent contesting the will would be wasted money. Moreover, during the time you spent contesting it, there would be nothing at all forthcoming to you, though of course the brothers' shares would not be affected by your actions.'

Susan offered no argument. Thinking his advice taken, the little man obtained the signatures necessary on the various documents. He explained one or two matters regarding Craywood to Carlton. In a short time, he took his leave. With nods of embarrassment, the Stoddards left in his wake.

Gaye saw that the rain was falling with increased force outside the window. It was nothing, however, to the storm that was brewing inside. Susan got up and went to the desk where a decanter and glasses sat on a tray. She poured a glass to the brim and drank deeply of it. She looked like a spring stretched taut to its limits.

It was Carlton who broke the long silence. He spoke politely and with what sounded like genuine pity. He seemed to recognize the extent of Susan's humiliation.

'I'm sorry,' he said to her back.

She whirled on him. 'He changed that will. You know that's not what it originally said.'

'Yes, he did change it,' Carlton admitted. 'Only a few months ago. He talked to me about it. He said he felt that you did not love him, only his wealth. He was afraid you were going to leave him.'

Susan drank more of the amber liquid. When she did not reply, Carlton went on. 'You may not believe me, but I told Walter I thought he was being unfair. Regardless of how you did or did not love him, I thought as his wife you were entitled to more than he was giving you. I think so still.' He paused for a moment. 'I've already arranged to have your trust fund doubled, out of my own money. As for the house, you already have the right to live here if you wish. I expect to be travelling in the future, so you needn't worry about getting along with me.'

Far from being pleased by his words, Susan seemed angrier than ever. When she spoke, she fairly spat her words at him.

'Charity?' she said. 'You think I want your charity? I should have had it all, everything, and you offer me a few extra thousand dollars a year?'

'You stupid creature.' It was Dennis who spoke. They were the first words he had spoken since he had wheeled his chair into the room. 'If it were up to me, you'd be out of here bag and baggage by now. You ought to be grateful for what you're getting.'

Susan turned her wide, flashing eyes on him. She went livid. For a full minute she seemed unable to get any words from her throat, so contorted was she with rage.

'You . . . you . . . ' She could seem to find no words dreadful enough. 'You're not even half a man.' With a violent gesture she threw the rest of her drink into his face.

Gaye jumped to her feet, stunned by the scene. She had never dreamed Susan capable of such cruelty. They remained as they were, frozen in place, as seconds ticked by. Then, with an expression on his face of such hatred as Gaye had never seen before, Dennis whirled about in his chair and went swiftly from the room. Carlton shot a furious glance at Susan and rushed wordlessly after his brother.

Gaye found her voice at last. 'Susan, have you gone mad?' she asked.

But she underestimated her sister's fury. With no one else against whom to direct it, Susan turned now on her.

'You shut up,' she shrieked. 'I'm sick of you, sick of all your nonsense. I know what you'll say, you'll tell me how kind and generous Carlton is being. Do you think I don't know you're in love with him? Do you think I can't see that you've turned against me too?'

Gaye turned crimson. She shook her head. 'That's not true,' she cried.

Susan broke into sobs. 'Oh, let me

alone, let me alone,' she sobbed. She pushed violently past her sister and ran into the hall. The front door crashed open.

Gaye ran after her. As she watched from the steps, Susan ran toward the woods, dark in the rain. 'Susan, wait, come back,' Gaye yelled, but Susan ran on as though she were possessed.

Gaye turned toward the stairs, thinking of Carlton, of asking him to help her bring Susan back, but she stopped. Carlton and Dennis were furious with Susan. She could hardly expect them to go out into the rain after her, and even if either of them would do so, they would only add to Susan's hysteria.

She raced to the closet and yanked out two raincoats, throwing one about her shoulder. Outside, Susan had already disappeared into the woods. Her heart pounding in her chest, Gaye ran after her.

10

Although it was still afternoon, the thickness of the woods and the rain overhead gave an illusion of night. Incongruously, Gaye had the thought that she had wanted from the beginning to explore these woods.

'Susan,' she called aloud, plunging through the undergrowth. There was no sight of her sister, nor was there a discernible path to follow. Gaye circled trees and the thickest bushes, heedless of her direction. Her uncovered hair was already dripping rainwater. It was a cold, unpleasant place to be. 'Susan.'

She paused, breathing heavily, and listened. She thought she heard someone crashing through the brush ahead and to her left. She ran in that direction, but the noise eluded her. She paused again, but there were only forest sounds now.

'Susan?' She looked this way and that in a near panic. How far could Susan have gone? She had had only a minute or two advantage, surely she could not have just disappeared. No wood was that thick.

But, Gaye reminded herself, Susan probably knew this forest well. *For all I know*, she thought, *she might be in some sheltered favourite spot right now, dry and comfortable and stubbornly refusing to answer*. That would be not unlike Susan, too.

Something moved far to her right, but she could not see it. 'Susan?' she asked in a smaller voice. Fear was like a leaden weight within her. She had an urge to run hysterically, to scream, to let her fear out. With an effort of will she held herself where she was for a moment longer, trying to collect her senses.

She could not find Susan herself, certainly not if Susan were not answering her calls. And if there were danger in these woods, she herself would not suffice to avert it. The thing to do was to return to the house and get Carlton. No matter how angry he was, surely he would listen to her pleas.

Unless . . . but she pushed that 'unless'

aside. He must help her find Susan, and if he absolutely refused, there was still one possibility left. There were guns in the house. Armed, she would better be able to face whatever threats this forest held.

Only, she did not know where the house was. Without paths, unfamiliar with the landmarks, unable to see Craywood, she had again lost all sense of direction. She ran in one direction for a moment, but the woods only seemed thicker. She ran to the side. Then again she stopped.

I mustn't panic, she thought. She was literally gasping for air now, both from fear and from exertion. Again there were sounds in the brush. She stifled a scream.

A scream came nonetheless. It was not hers, but Susan's, and it was a cry of pure horror. It came again and again, the terrified bleating of a doomed creature.

'Susan!' Gaye panicked. She began to run blindly, calling Susan's name, ignoring the branches that ripped the plastic off her raincoat and scraped her skin. Her eyes filled with tears, so that she could hardly see where she was going. 'Susan, Susan,' she sobbed over and over.

For a moment she had followed the direction of the screams but now, horribly, they were ended. The forest was silent except for her own sobbing and the sounds of her flight. She stumbled once and fell into wet grass and mud. She had a premonition of death, and for a fleeting second she surrendered to it, sobbing weakly into the water-soaked earth.

'Oh, God, help me,' she thought. She shook her clinging wet hair from her face and scrambled to her feet. Susan, where was Susan, what had happened to her? She must find her. She ran on, no longer screaming or sobbing.

She burst suddenly into an opening. Before her were two or three feet of soft grass, and a gully that sloped sharply downward for several yards to a small stream that ran muddy brown. There, on the stream's bank, lay Susan, arms and legs askew. Her dress and her flesh were splotched with blood that the rain had turned into little rivulets.

And there, leaning over her, his hand at her throat, as streaked with blood as she was, was Carlton.

Gaye screamed once, a senseless high-pitched shriek of anguish. She ran blindly toward them, sobbing again. A tree root caught her foot and she was suddenly tumbling and rolling, over the hill, down the ravine, over and over, until the blackness closed in about her.

★ ★ ★

Gradually the darkness receded. The fear did not rush in at once to fill the vacancy. She was left briefly with that hollow sensation that is part of unfeeling.

She became aware first of the cold, seeming to chill the very marrow in her bones. Then came the realization that someone was holding her. She was in the embrace of strong arms, her head resting against a broad, solid chest. A gentle hand stroked her cheek.

At last came memory, and with it the fear rushed back. Her eyes flew open and she found herself staring into Carlton's handsome face. Seized with panic, she struggled against him, trying to bring a fresh scream from her lungs, but he held

173

her tight, and as the wave of panic passed through her, she looked into his eyes and saw that there was no threat there, only tender concern. She ceased to struggle. Her head hurt so. She was so cold, and his arm about her felt warm and secure . . .

She jerked herself stiffly back to consciousness, flinging her eyes open once again to meet his. His face was closer, only inches from hers, so close that she could scarcely focus on his features.

'Don't you know I could never hurt you,' he said in a voice so soft and low that she might almost have overheard his thoughts.

It was all too much for her to comprehend. She knew she must fear him. She knew that he was in some way dangerous. She knew that he had lied to the Sheriff and used her feeling for him to persuade her to lie as well.

And he had attacked Susan. Hadn't she seen him with her own eyes? But she did not want to know these things. What she wanted to know was the feeling of peace and warmth that his arms gave her, the sense of belonging that passed through her when she saw the gentle concern in his eyes.

She tried again to put her thoughts in order. 'Susan?' she asked feebly.

'She's alive,' he said. 'She's hurt, though.' When she said nothing, only stared up at him, he added, 'I'm sorry, truly.'

She tried to sit up. He helped her. Beyond him she could see Susan, still where she had been before, but his coat, a dark mackinaw, was over her. Except for the chilling rain and a pool of blood that the coat did not conceal, she might have been asleep.

'I'll have to get her back to the house,' he said, 'but I couldn't leave you here unconscious. Can you walk all right?'

'I don't know.' She tried, with his help, to get up. A lightning flash of pain shot up from one ankle. She looked down to see that it had already started to swell.

'I think I can make it,' she said. She tried to take a step, but the pain was too intense. Despite her will, the leg gave under her and she fell against him.

'No good,' he said. He helped her back to the ground in the shelter of a huge boulder that kept some of the rain from them. She saw that he wore nothing but shirt and trousers and they were long since soaked. They clung to his body coldly, and she realized how chilled he must be. She had come out with another raincoat, but she had lost it somewhere in the woods. The one she wore was in shreds, so that she was only slightly drier than he was.

He looked anxiously from her to Susan, and back to her. 'I can't carry you both at once,' he said, trying to smile, but she saw how worried he was, and she understood. If he had not attacked Susan, then whoever or whatever had was still in these woods. Whichever of them he left behind was in danger of another attack.

Despite the fear gnawing at her stomach, she said, 'You'll have to take her and come back for me, it seems.'

'I can't leave you here alone.'

'Better me conscious than her unconscious,' she said. When he still hesitated, she said, 'Please, hurry, the longer you

176

wait the worse it is. I'll be all right, I promise.'

He seemed to realize she was right. He had tucked a pistol into his belt, and he took it out now and handed it to her. 'Can you use one?' he asked.

She nodded. 'My father taught me when I was just a little tomboy.'

They exchanged wan smiles. He looked around. 'I'm afraid I'm going to have to make you still more uncomfortable,' he said. He picked her up easily in his arms and carried her toward the stream, sitting her finally right at its edge. She was close enough that she could have dangled her fingers in its swift current if she wanted. She was out of the protection of the boulder, nor were there trees within several feet, and she was at the mercy of the steady rain, but she could also see for yards in any direction.

'If anything should happen,' he said, speaking in a voice that discouraged questions, 'go into the stream. If you can, put it between you and . . . and anything that might come along, but at least, get into the water.'

She did not understand, but she nodded. 'And,' he added, 'use the gun. Regardless.'

He gave her a last, long look. Then he stood and went swiftly to where he had left Susan. He lifted her in his arms, covering her as best he could with the mackinaw.

'I'll get back as fast as I possibly can,' he said over his shoulder. Then he was off, loping across the ground in a fast trot. She watched him until he had disappeared into the forest.

The silence closed in around her. The aloneness was overpowering. Her every sense was raw with awareness of the forest about. The scent of damp earth, the odour of things growing and things decaying, clung to her. What had seemed silence was a cacophony of forest noises — the rushing of the stream beside her, the rustle of leaves and twigs, the steady drip, drip, drip of the rain. The ground was hard and wet and cold to her touch. Even her mouth was filled with the taste of earth and rain.

She looked from side to side, eyes

straining to catch any unusual sight. The woods played games with her. She would see a flash of colour there for an instant and then it was gone. A strange new sound would intrude upon the ones gradually growing familiar, and fade again. Her head throbbed. She lifted a hand to one temple and brought it back flecked with blood. She must have hurt her head when she fell.

She thought again of that first glimpse of Susan and Carlton. When he had been here, holding her, speaking to her in that comforting baritone voice of his, she had been certain that she was mistaken in her initial impression, that Carlton had attacked Susan. Carlton was not an attacker, but a rescuer. Hadn't he left the gun with her, hadn't he been concerned for her safety?

For her safety, yes — he had said that he could never hurt her. But what of Susan? No, he had carried Susan to safety — *or had he?*

Alone, fear played with her thoughts. Perhaps Carlton *had* attacked Susan. Perhaps only her arrival on the scene had saved Susan's life.

If Susan were alive. Suppose Susan 'died' on the way back to the house. There would even be her own testimony that Carlton had tried to save Susan, tried to save them both. Susan was already bruised and cut up. Another blow would not be evident.

Stop it, she told herself. That was the path, surely, to panic. She had to believe Carlton, she had to believe that he would take Susan safely to the house and return for her.

But if he didn't? What could she do? As though driven by the thought, she tried again to get to her feet, but the burning pain in her ankle became a stabbing agony as soon as she tried to use it. She thought of using a stick to support her weight, but even to find one, she would have to make it into the woods, and she could only do that by crawling.

The minutes seemed to stand still. Even Time mocked her. She looked at her watch. Time was standing still. The watch had stopped. Furious, she shook it and lifted it to her ear. It was running again.

The faint ticking spoke to her: Carlton, it said, Carlton, Carlton.

She knew that terror was overpowering her, and she knew she must fight it, because if once it had hold of her, a complete hold of her, she would be helpless in its grasp. Surely Carlton would be back soon, in a few minutes, just a few more minutes, if only she could remain calm. A few more minutes.

'I'll think of pleasant things,' she thought with determination. She looked around her again. It was a pretty spot. On a sunny day it would be exquisite. She loved the out-of-doors. She imagined the stream running pure and crystal clear, with little fish darting about, and perhaps tadpoles. She thought of the flowers that bloomed all around here and there through the trees.

There was a crashing in the brush, the sound of something approaching. Her heart seemed to stop. Her grasp tightened on the gun. She remembered what Carlton had told her and began to scramble into the stream. It was cold and fast-moving, but not deep. She was able to crawl into the middle, holding the gun up to keep it dry. Her eyes were wide with terror. She braced herself against the stream's current and stared at the woods.

A glimpse of something approaching — she lifted the gun, but it was Carlton who burst into view. He saw the gun lifted toward him and stopped short.

'Easy,' he called out, 'it's only me.' He realized then that she was in the stream, and looked sharply about. 'Are you all right?'

She let the gun slip from her fingers. It splashed into the water. 'Oh, Carlton,' was all she could say. Then she began to cry.

He was with her in a minute, lifting her from the icy water. He had brought a blanket and he wrapped it carefully around her. Then, carrying her as easily as if she weighed nothing, he set out a second time toward the house, running in long strides. She clung to him, her face buried against his chest.

'You're soaked through,' she said, feeling the wetness of his shirt.

He said nothing, conserving his breath.

She realized that he must have run all the way to the house and back for her. He must be exhausted and cold. He hadn't even taken time to change his clothes or get himself a coat, only to grab a blanket for her.

She clung the more tightly to him. She knew that no matter what, she loved him, as she had never loved before and could never love again. Of everything else, she was uncertain, but of this, she was quite sure.

Stoddard came out to meet them, carrying his shotgun. Carlton's pace was slower now. Gaye could hear the pounding of his heart against her ear and the laboured strain of his breathing, but when Stoddard offered to take her, Carlton declined, kept her in his own strong arms. She knew she ought to insist, that he must be nearly at the limits of his strength, but she said nothing.

Louise, looking not far from hysteria herself, was waiting at the open door. Carlton carried Gaye straight to her room, depositing her wetly atop the bed.

'The doctor will come,' Louise told him.

Carlton was breathing hard. 'Louise will help you get into bed,' he said.

'Susan . . . ?' she asked.

'She's all right. She's in bed already.'

Although her suspicions turned her cheeks crimson, she had to ask, 'She's alive?'

The softness of his expression hardened as the implication of her question hit home. 'Yes,' he said shortly.

'You'd better go get out of those things,' she said after a long, awkward pause. 'You'll be lucky if you don't have pneumonia by this time.'

'Yes,' he said again. He looked long and searchingly at her. She wished she could say to him something of what was in her heart, but Louise was here, bringing hot towels, helping her get her shoes off.

He seemed to understand. The look of tenderness came back to his eyes. Then something so unexpected and so wonderful happened that she could scarcely believe it had occurred at all. Louise turned from them for a moment. Carlton's eyes held Gaye's, and his lips moved. The words were scarcely more than a whisper, but to her it was as though he had shouted them from across the room.

'I love you,' he said. Then, without waiting for an answer, he turned from her and left the room.

With Louise's help, she got undressed and managed a hot bath. By the time the doctor arrived, she was in bed, sporting a large bandage around her head and a heap of warm towels wrapped about her ankle.

'Have you examined my sister?' she asked as soon as he entered the room. 'She's more serious than I am.'

'Yes, I've already looked at her,' he assured her, beginning to examine her ankle. 'She'll be all right in time. She's a lucky girl, though.'

'Lucky?' She winced as he pressed into the swollen flesh.

'She's the first one to live through an attack by those wolves. All the others were killed and torn apart. She's got a couple of bad wounds, and she's lost a lot of blood, but aside from that, she'll be all right.'

Gaye lay quietly and let him feel and probe. She tried not to think about his remarks, but they would not be put aside.

Wolves? But she had been in the woods too, and she had neither seen nor heard wolves, nor had she been attacked. She had seen and heard nothing, except . . . except Carlton.

'Don't you know I could never hurt you?' he had said, and in her memory, she added emphasis to the 'you.'

She covered her face with her hands so that the doctor could not see her torment. 'Oh, Carlton,' she prayed, 'let me believe you, let me know that you are innocent.' But the prayer was unanswered.

11

She slept as though drugged — and indeed, she thought when she awoke, she probably had been. It was morning. She had slept away the rest of the day and all of the night.

She started to get up and open her shutters before she remembered her ankle. Annoyed, she leaned back against the head-board. She did not like being confined, but the doctor had said the sprain was not bad, and after a day or two in bed, she would be able to get around with a cane. There was nothing to do but resign herself to the situation.

Louise came in a little while to bring her breakfast and help her to freshen up, and shortly afterward, Carlton came to see her. He made no reference to his parting remark of the previous day, but she saw that there was a hesitancy about him that was unlike his usual brash manner. It was, although she would never have imagined it possible, as though he were suddenly very shy with her.

They spoke in an oddly impersonal manner for a few moments, but when she asked about Susan, his face darkened.

'She's going to be all right,' he said. 'The doctor said there was no need to send her to a hospital, but she will be confined to bed for several days. I've arranged for a nurse to come in and look after the both of you.'

'Carlton, what is it?' she asked. 'There's something you're not telling me.'

He avoided her eyes, looking instead at the floor. 'Did you get a good look at her, there in the woods?' he asked.

'No, I was . . . I wasn't exactly myself when I came to where you . . . where she was. And when I woke up, I couldn't think clearly at all.'

He smiled affectionately at the bandage on her head. 'You had a pretty nasty bump. We're just lucky there was no concussion or anything like that.'

'Carlton?' She knew he was avoiding whatever unpleasant information he had for her.

His smile faded but he did not look away this time. 'The doctor says she's going to be badly scarred,' he said.

Gaye caught her breath. She thought of her beautiful sister, and could not help but remember how very vain Susan was, how she had always relied upon her beauty to get her way. She was filled with pity for the unhappiness Susan would experience.

'How awful,' she said finally.

'I want you to understand,' he said, 'whatever I can do, I will. It's still too early of course to know what will be possible with plastic surgery, but when the time comes to consider that, I don't want you to concern yourself with the expense. Craywood will pay for everything.'

'Thank you,' she said. She touched his hand with her fingertips. He clasped her hand in his and lifted it to his lips, kissing it gently.

She had come to a decision before he had joined her and he had to be told about it. 'Carlton,' she said, 'I've decided when Susan is able to move, I'm going to 'insist on taking her away from here.'

'Where will you go?' he asked.

'I don't know. Probably back to Los Angeles.'

'Will you be gone permanently?'

'I . . . I don't know that either.' She wished that she could say something else, but she had promised herself to be honest about this. She knew that, as much as Susan, she needed to be away from Craywood. Especially, she needed to be away from Carlton, to think over everything that had happened to her and make some decisions of her own. She could not make them here, not with any confidence.

'I see,' was all he said, but he could not hide his disappointment.

The nurse arrived that same morning. She divided her time between Susan and Gaye, although Gaye needed less attention. In another day, Gaye was able to hobble around with the help of a fancy cane Carlton had brought her. Her first trip was to see Susan.

She had tried to prepare herself for the visit, and she thought she had, but when she looked for the first time upon Susan's face, she could not completely hide her shock.

Susan smiled bitterly at her. 'Yes, hideous isn't it?' she said. 'And to think, darling sister, I once pitied you because you weren't beautiful.'

'Susan,' Gaye said, summoning her self control, 'you're making a mountain out of a molehill. After what you went through, of course there would be some bruises, probably some scars, but I don't see anything that looks like it will be really permanent. And if there is, well, don't forget that they can do almost anything with plastic surgery these days. Take my word for it, six months from now, there will be no sign of any of this.'

Susan smiled and did not argue the point, but her eyes said she did not believe it, any more than Gaye herself did. Gaye made small talk, trying to cheer Susan, and she told her as well of her intention to leave Craywood as soon as they were able.

'Very well,' Susan said.

Gaye had expected an argument, but

there was something ominous in Susan's quiet acceptance. It was too quick, too disinterested.

'We can take our time driving down the coast,' Gaye went on, painting as attractive a picture as she could. 'Spend a few days in San Francisco, and then stop off at Monterey. It's as beautiful as ever. A few days there and you'll feel like you've been born anew.'

'I'm sure,' Susan said. 'And if nothing else, I should certainly provide the tourists with something to gawk at. We could even turn a little profit. You could charge people to come see the scarred lady.'

'Susan,' Gaye cried.

Susan dismissed her protest with a wave of her hand. 'Don't be a fool, do you think I haven't looked in the mirror a thousand times, do you think I'm so stupid as to think this is all just going to go away.'

She lit a cigarette. Gaye could think of nothing more to say. Susan puffed on the cigarette for a moment. 'I think,' she said, sounding calmer, 'that it's retribution for all my wickedness.'

'But you haven't been wicked,' Gaye argued. 'Foolish, yes, vain and head-strong, but if everyone were punished for that sort of thing, we'd all be in bandages.'

Susan managed a smile. 'Dear sweet Gaye, if only life and the people in it were as nice as you see them.'

But for all her protests, Gaye could not completely put away the idea that perhaps Susan was right, perhaps she had lost her beauty as retribution for her vanity and her selfishness of the past.

If so, although it caused her bitterness and grief in the present, it might eventually help her to become a better person. She hoped so. She had not liked the person Susan had become. She wanted to believe that beneath the hard shell Susan had acquired in the last few years was the charming and delightful girl she had known before. If this incident had served to crack that shell, then it was not a complete tragedy — but she kept these thought to herself.

One point lingered in her mind,

however, and at last she asked Susan about it. 'Did you see who or what it was that attacked you?'

'No,' Susan answered, shaking her head. 'Something sprang upon me from behind. That's all that I remember until I woke up in my bed.' After a thoughtful moment, she smiled more warmly than before, and said, 'I understand you came to rescue me.'

'I'm afraid I didn't do much good,' Gaye said.

'Perhaps. Who knows what might have happened to me if you hadn't been around. I may owe my life to your bravery.'

'You wouldn't call me brave if you had seen me,' Gaye insisted with a grin. 'I was a positive ninny.'

* * *

Within a few days, Gaye was able to get around without her cane. At her insistence the nurse was dismissed, and Gaye looked after Susan herself. The doctor came and went. Susan was better. She would be up and around in a few more days. In answer to Gaye's question, the doctor suggested she shouldn't travel for at least another week.

Although Gaye was busy, the days were relatively uneventful. There were no further tragedies to mar their lives, and this period of peace was so in contrast to what had gone before that it seemed almost pleasant. Gaye could almost forget the tragedies that had befallen them, and the gloomy atmosphere of Craywood.

Almost, but not quite. She did not venture out of the house, not even onto her little terrace. Those doors were kept carefully bolted at all times. At night she kept the shutters closed. She did not want to think of any eyes in the darkness beyond, watching her.

The Stoddards still left before sundown each evening. During Gaye's time in bed, Louise had looked after her as much as the nurse had. She had fussed over her and shown in a hundred little ways that she had taken a liking to Gaye.

Gaye could see, however, whenever she looked at her, that Louise was still as beset by fear and anxiety as she had ever been. Her nerves were taut. The slightest sound or unexpected movement made her start as though in utter terror. She had a habit of looking over her shoulder every minute or so, and when she left a room, she peeked into the hall first, to assure herself that it was safe. Her nervousness was contagious, so that, although she liked Louise, Gaye could not help being ill at ease when she was around.

When Gaye was able to get around with the cane, Louise voiced her fears to her one morning. 'You will leave Craywood now, eh?' she said as Gaye helped herself to some coffee one morning.

'As soon as my sister is able to go,' Gaye said. 'We're going to take a trip south.'

Louise gave her a frightened look. 'No, no,' she said in a low voice. 'You must go now. Send for her when she is well, but go now.'

Gaye laughed off the warning. 'Nonsense, I can't go without my sister. Besides, there is nothing to be afraid of if we stay inside.'

'The *loukerouk*,' Louise said, casting a

glance over her shoulder as though that word might conjure up some demon.

'The what?' Gaye had never heard the word before.

Louise leaned closer across the buffet and spoke in a still lower voice. 'The *loukerouk*,' she said. 'This house will not save you from the *loukerouk*. You must go, quickly.'

'I don't know what you mean?' Despite her determination to remain calm, Gaye felt herself gripped by fear.

'It is nearly the time of the full moon,' Louise said hoarsely. 'That is the worst of all. Go, while there is still time.'

'I don't understand any of this,' Gaye said, shaking her head. 'I don't know what a *loukerouk* is, and I can't imagine what the moon has to do with anything.'

Before Louise could say more, Carlton strode into the room. Louise went silent at once and with a sullen look in his direction, slipped into the kitchen.

'You look glum this morning,' he said from his end of the table.

She managed a smile. 'Louise seems to think I'm going to be eaten alive in my bed,' she said. She had meant it to sound funny, but Carlton did not seem to find it so. She was on the verge of asking him about the word Louise had used, and thought better of it.

A few days after that, when Gaye was getting around without even the help of a cane, Louise came one afternoon to her room. It was late in the day, time for Louise to be leaving, and for Gaye to be looking after their dinner.

'I brought you this,' Louise said, pressing something into Gaye's hand.

Gaye looked at it. It was a charm of some sort on a silver chain. The charm itself was like a wire ball that contained a brown, resinous looking substance. Gaye lifted it to her nose and sniffed. The scent was acrid, reminiscent of garlic and onion, with some herbs she could not identify.

'What is it?' she asked. She thought it a highly unpleasant gift, although the silver was old and attractively worked.

'Devil's dung,' was the answer

'Oh.' Gaye could not think what one was to do with anything that smelled so bad and with such a dreadful name.

'You must wear it,' Louise explained, pointing to Gaye's throat. 'You must wear it at all times.'

'I see.' Not wanting to hurt the woman's feelings, Gaye slipped the chain about her throat, letting the silver charm drop across her breast. She had to restrain herself from wrinkling up her nose at the smell.

'Wear it always,' Louise insisted. 'It is a charm against the *loukerouk*. It is the strongest I know, but you must never, never take it off, not even for a moment.'

Gaye could not help thinking life would be a great deal less pleasant if she had to wear this little silver charm forever, but Louise's words gave her a chill.

'Louise,' she said, 'Tell me about this, what do you call it, this 'loukalouk'.'

'The *loukerouk*, he is not done, and you are so good. Oh, please leave this place, go now.' She began to cry.

'Oh, don't cry,' Gaye said, putting out her hand to pat Louise's shoulder, but the unexpected touch only made the Cajun jump.

'The *loukerouk*,' she said again and, peering into the hall first, she slipped from the room.

Gaye stared after her a moment, but the odour of the charm again captured her attention. She took it from around her throat and studied it. Yes, it was very old, probably something handed down through generations of Louise's ancestors. Louise was Cajun, one of those half French inhabitants of the deep South's bayous. Beliefs in strange demons and monsters were probably still strong among them, and they would turn to other forms of magic to protect them from the imaginary evils. This charm had probably comforted countless simple folk over the years.

She looked more closely at the substance held in the wire mesh. Some sort of resin, yes, she was certain of that. Devil's dung. She'd never heard the phrase, but probably it too came from the shadowy backwaters of the bayou.

The smell was less noticeable as the time passed. She wondered if it could have faded so quickly, then dismissed that idea, telling herself that she was probably just getting used to it.

And next thing, she added, laughing at her own foolishness, *I'll have myself convinced that I should wear it to fend off the goblins.*

There was a knock at the door. Carlton came in to ask a question about dinner. He was about to go when he noticed the charm that she still held in her hand.

'What's that?' he asked.

'A charm of some sort,' she said, handing him the silver ornament.

He examined it closely and sniffed at it. 'Assafoetida,' he said.

'Devil's dung?'

'The same. Where did you get it?'

She hesitated for a second, but she could think of no reason to conceal the truth from him. 'Louise gave it to me,' she said. 'She seemed to think it would protect me from danger. According to her instructions, I'm to wear it at all times and never, never take it off.'

She tried to make a joke of it, but he seemed not amused. 'Maybe she's right,' he said. He gave it back to her. 'See you at dinner.'

She stood for a while at her window, staring at the terrace. What was it that Louise feared? Both Louise and Dennis had warned her to leave, that she was not safe, even in the house, but of what was she to be afraid? Or of whom?

She did not wear the charm when she went to take care of dinner, but neither did she leave it behind. It was in her pocket, neatly wrapped in tissue.

12

Dinner was a somewhat slower process now. She had to take meals to both Dennis and Susan. Not until they were both served could she sit down to dine with Carlton.

This was the event of her day toward which she looked each morning. For all of her suspicions and uncertainties, Carlton had come to be the most important element of her life.

Nor was he unaware of this, she felt certain. He was, during these evening interludes, a different person. He was charming and pleasant and witty. It was as if he set out each evening to prove to her how likable he could be. Every serious discussion or worry was forgotten for the better part of an hour. Gaye found herself thinking they might have been a married couple, taking their evening meal together each evening.

Afterward, he retired to his rooms.

Without sounding very critical of his brother, he had let her know that Walter had not managed the Cray estates so very well after all. Not, he had been careful to stress, that they were in any sort of difficulty, but it seemed much had been neglected, errors in accounting had been left uncorrected, important papers had been misplaced, correspondence unanswered.

With the estate now his responsibility, Carlton was working hard to put things in order, and he devoted this evening time to his chores.

Gaye had never been at a loss to amuse herself. Sometimes she visited with Susan, or she would read, or perhaps only settle herself in front of the fire in the den, to muse.

This evening, however, she went into the library. The dictionary told her that assafoetida was indeed a resin, and that it was also known as Devil's dung, and that it had certain medicinal properties. It offered nothing regarding any magical properties the resin might possess.

She could find no entry at all under *loukerouk*, although she checked every spelling she could think of. She was poring over the dictionary, trying to think of any other possible way to spell the word when Carlton came in.

'Homework?' he asked, taking down a book he had come for.

'Just a word that puzzled me,' she said. She did not know whether she should repeat Louise's warning to Carlton. She might be causing trouble for the cook.

'What is it, maybe I can help,' he said, adding with a grin, 'Not that I'm any intellectual, but it just might be something I know about.'

She took a deep breath. 'I was trying to find the word *loukerouk*,' she said.

He seemed to take a long time to speak. 'Where did you hear that word?' he asked.

'From Louise. She warned me to beware of the *loukerouk*, but I've never heard the word before, and I can't seem to find it in the dictionary.'

His rack of pipes was on the desk top. He busied himself with filling one and lighting it. The aroma of burning tobacco, masculine and intimate, drifted to her.

'It's a bastardization of the French. *Loup-garou*.'

'*Loup-garou?*' For a moment the phrase suggested nothing to her.

'Werewolf,' he explained simply.

The room seemed to turn suddenly cold. Gaye shivered. Instinctively her hand went to the pocket that held the charm. It was still there.

She tried to laugh but her throat was dry and the sound came out hoarse and unnatural. 'I see,' she said. 'Of course I should have expected Louise would believe in something like that. Well, I don't have to worry about it now, do I?'

'Why is that?'

'I've no reason to be afraid of something that doesn't exist.'

'Are you so sure that it doesn't?' he asked.

'Aren't you?'

He strode to the window, staring out at the moonlit grounds. Gaye could not prevent herself from thinking that it was nearly the full moon. Werewolves, so the stories said, prowled during the full moon. And Louise had warned her of the moon. 'That is the worst of all,' she had said. Because the *loukerouk* prowled?

'No matter how reasonable or scientific we try to be,' Carlton said, speaking with his back to her, 'Man has never been able to shed the werewolf legends. Of all those monsters and demons and spirits that haunt our nightmares and folklore and literature, the werewolf is king. None other is mentioned so often or with such terror. He is everywhere. In Italy he's the *lupo manaro*. In Spain, they call him *lob ombre*, in Portugal, *lob omem*. In Germany he's *wer-wolf*, and the French seem to have had a superabundance of the *loup-garou*. Do you think all those people, over all the world, through all those centuries, have been completely wrong?'

'There must . . . there must be logical explanations.'

'Oh, yes, of course. In the first place, man has regarded the wolf as a deadly enemy since the dawn of history — vicious predators, prowling in packs, eating whatever meat they can find, including human flesh. Do you know that men hunt other dangerous animals to control them, but when it comes to the wolf, men have tried over the centuries to wipe them out completely, to exterminate them? They've succeeded, too, in many places, but the wolf still has his domain. A pack was seen in France in 1963. It caused international headlines. And a man was attacked in Canada the same year. Italy, Spain, Portugal, Turkey, Poland — they've all had sightings in the last few years.'

'Walter said there were none in the States,' she said.

'That's right, not in decades, except for Alaska.'

But if not, she thought, what is it that has prowled these woods, killing, mauling, howling?

'Picture the beast himself,' Carlton went on. 'He's eerie. If ever an animal looked supernatural, it's the wolf.'

Gaye made a mental picture of the wolf — a creature of the night, a vague grey colour, the eyes catlike, glowing, red in firelight, yellow in moonlight — and the ghostly wailing. It was true, no other animal aroused such unreasonable fear in one. Was it some primitive knowledge remaining in the race consciousness, warning of things too evil to understand?

'They became associated with witches in the middle ages, didn't they?' she asked aloud.

'Sometimes. Sometimes they were thought to be witches with the power of metamorphosis, or changing shape. And sometimes the werewolf was just a werewolf. Sometimes a man became one accidentally, drinking water from which wolves had drunk, or eating a certain plant. And sometimes a man had to employ a ritual.'

'You mean, become a werewolf intentionally?'

He turned to look at her. He seemed transformed by the subject. He might have been talking to himself, or thinking aloud. She tried to avoid wondering how he had come to be such an authority on this odd subject.

'Does that shock you?' he asked. 'Oh, yes, men sometimes want to become werewolves. There's a very elaborate ritual for it, as eerie as anything black magic has to offer. One must go to a special sort of

209

place, a hilltop for instance, or best of all, a lonely wood. Such as Craywood.'

He came closer, speaking in a low, intense voice. 'On the night of the full moon, at midnight, he will draw the magic circle . . . '

As he talked on, the room seemed to recede from Gaye and she could almost see the horrid ritual being acted out. As Carlton described it for her, in that hypnotic tone, the steps were played upon the stage of her imagination as surely as though she were present at such a ritual. The wide outer circle is formed first, seven feet in diameter. Within that, the lone man makes another circle, this one three feet in diameter, and within the smaller circle he builds a fire, its flames bright against the blackness of the forest, its wood snapping and hissing ominously. The cauldron is put over the fire and brought to boil, and into it goes those dread ingredients of black magic, hemlock and parsley, opium and henbane, and others too grim to contemplate.

'The supplicant's voice rises in incantation,' Carlton said, his voice casting a spell. ''Wolves, vampires, satyrs, ghosts! Elect of all the devilish hosts! I pray you send hither, send hither, send hither, The great grey shape that makes men shiver!' As he chants, he strips naked, and smears himself with an ointment he has prepared beforehand, a thick, obnoxious substance that contains dead cats as well as magical herbs. And, finally, the most solemn moment of all, the necessary donning of a wolf skin. He kneels, and the transformation begins . . . '

'Carlton, stop!' Gaye threw her hands over her face to break the spell. The horror of that devilish ceremony was too real. She had begun to tremble.

Carlton put an arm around her and led her to a chair. They were silent until he brought her a brandy.

'One of the most powerful charms against the werewolf is assafoetida,' he said, speaking now in his normal voice. 'That's why Louise gave you that charm.'

Something occurred to her. 'Is sulphur some sort of protection, too?' she asked.

'Yes, and henbane and wolfsbane, and clear spring water. And running water.'

She understood then, that was why he had told her to get into the stream when he had left her in the woods. And the sulphur and spring water at the Stoddard's cottage. She could understand their believing in legends from the old country, but Carlton? Surely he was too intelligent for that.

'Silver is protection too,' he went on, 'Especially in a crucifix. And of course, to kill a werewolf, you need silver bullets, especially those blessed in a chapel of Saint Hubert, the patron saint of hunters.'

The brandy had helped to restore her calm. She was able now to look at him directly. She thought that he was trying to tell her something more than just the history of the werewolf, the *loukerouk*. Perhaps he was trying actually to frighten her. Perhaps he wanted her to leave, as did the others, but could not bring himself to say it outright, and wanted to frighten her into making that decision.

She finished the drink. Carlton had grown silent. He smoked his pipe and studied her. He seemed to be waiting for her to come to some decision. Inwardly she was too confused to assimilate all of this, but she knew that to admit to a fear is to give it strength, give it control over you. You cannot overcome that to which you give service.

'It's all very intriguing,' she said, standing. 'You certainly seem knowledgeable on the subject.'

'I've read some,' he said.

'I see. Well, we can be grateful at least for one thing. If we're to be plagued with dark creatures, it's just as well that they are the imaginary kind.'

'Are you still so certain that they are?'

'What else could they be? You said yourself that there are no wolves in this country today.'

'I said no wolves. I didn't comment on the possibilities of werewolves.'

She started toward the door to the hall. 'I venture to say there are none of those either. With all your reading, I'll bet you can't cite me a single reported case of a werewolf in this country. Certainly not in this century.'

'The last reported case,' he said evenly, 'was on an Indian reservation in the West.

Navajo, I believe. He raided flocks, dug up graves, even killed and ate women.'

'And when was this?'

'1946.'

After a moment, she said, 'Good night, Carlton.'

'Gaye.' His voice stopped her again. She looked back to find him still studying her intently.

'Wear the charm that Louise gave you,' he said.

'Surely you don't believe that will protect me in some way,' she said skeptically.

'Indeed, I do. I very much believe it.'

She left him without further comment and went to her own room. She would have liked to believe that he was joking, playing some sort of game with her, but she did not think that. He had looked all too serious. However he had come to his conclusions, he thought that the silver charm would protect her.

But could she believe that? Her practical mind scoffed at the possibility. She could scarcely imagine that people in this day and age gave credence to werewolves — and yet, Louise and her husband certainly did, and Carlton seemed to. And Dennis, too, had warned her of wolves, the wolves of Craywood. A joke, Carlton had said, but was it? At least three people had died, set upon by some mysterious beast in the very woods outside this house. Susan had been attacked and badly mauled. She herself had heard the eerie howling of some animal, one sounding very much like a wolf.

She talked to herself as she made ready for bed. 'It's too silly,' she said aloud. '*Loukerouks* and werewolves and henbane.'

Nevertheless, she double checked the bolts on all the doors, and after she was in bed, she got up again and went to the closet and found the dress she had worn that evening. The silver charm was still in the pocket. She took it out and, bringing it back to the bed with her, put it under her pillow.

Whether due to the charm or no, she slept safely — that night, at least.

13

It did seem to her that the charm had lost much of its unpleasant odour when she examined it in the morning, and though she chided herself for her foolishness, she ended by putting it on before she left her room.

'If nothing else,' she said, admitting that she was only inventing excuses, 'it will keep Louise and Carlton from worrying.'

The reactions were a little disappointing, however. Louise seemed not to notice the charm. She was more preoccupied than usual, and Gaye's attempts to draw her into a conversation produced nothing more than a few monosyllables.

Susan did notice the charm. 'Good heavens, what smells so dreadful?' she demanded when Gaye brought her breakfast.

'I'm afraid it must be this,' Gaye admitted, showing her the charm.

'What is it?' Susan wrinkled her nose in distaste.

'A charm of some sort, to keep away the hobgoblins. It was a present from Louise.'

'Well, I don't know how you can stand to wear it. The smell makes me ill from all the way over here. Take it off, would you, and bury it somewhere.'

Gaye sighed and put the charm back into her pocket. She would have to remember not to wear it into Susan's room again.

The more she thought of it, though, the sillier it seemed to wear it at all, especially if the lessening of smell was only an illusion and it was still as strong to others. She hardly cared to have everyone thinking she chose to smell like that.

Before returning to the dining room, she went back to her bedroom and deposited the charm in her jewel box. Surely there it would keep her safe at night. In the daytime, she would simply have to rely on her own good sense.

Carlton did not appear for breakfast, but this was of no special consequence.

He often did not these days. He explained it as due to his working late in his room. Gaye suspected that he spent part of his night watching her room, but this was one of those matters she could not bring herself to discuss with Carlton.

She had a sense that they were biding time, but she did not know for what they waited. Since the attack on Susan, things had been actually peaceful, but Susan was better now. She was already able to get up and around by herself, although she had been warned against straining herself with climbing stairs or any serious walking.

The full moon was coming too. Gaye could not escape the feeling that they were building inexorably toward some climax. She railed against the blindness that would not let her see what the end was.

In the breakfast room she sat and thought of her strange conversation with Carlton. How real and terrifying he had managed to make his description of that primitive ceremony. She had actually had the sense of being there. A nagging suspicion asked if perhaps he had been present at such a ceremony, to have been able to describe it in such vivid detail, but she gave this no credence. What reason could he have for witnessing such a thing? What reason could anyone have for attending a ceremony of that sort? If you looked at it coldly, the whole thing was preposterous.

It was no less ominous, though, for being preposterous. In her mind's eye she saw again the flames leaping upward about a cauldron. She thought of the chant Carlton had quoted, the appeal to the Devil.

'I pray you,' she murmured, 'send hither, send hither, send hither, the great grey shape that makes men shiver . . . '

A loud crash broke her train of thought. She had not realized that she had spoken aloud, nor had she known that Louise had started into the room just then bearing a large tray of fresh rolls. Now the rolls and the tray were on the floor and Louise stood clinging to the doorframe, her eyes wide with terror.

'Louise, what on earth . . . ?' Gaye began, jumping to her feet.

'The *loukerouk*,' Louise cried, cringing from her, 'You summon the *loukerouk*!'

She realized then that Louise had heard the old chant and had recognized it. Louise thought she was using it to summon the devil. 'No, no,' she said, trying to take hold of the old woman. 'I was only repeating something I'd heard before.'

'*Dieu*,' Louise cried, stumbling back into the kitchen to escape her grasp. 'Save me, Father!'

'Louise.' Gaye went after her, but as she came into the kitchen, an iron skillet narrowly missed her head, crashing into the door instead. She froze in her tracks, scarcely able to believe that Louise had turned so violent.

Louise threw open the door to the outside and ran out. Before Gaye could follow her, Carlton came in from the breakfast room.

'What on earth's happening?' he demanded. 'It sounded like we were being bombarded.'

'It's Louise,' Gaye said. 'She heard me quoting that chant, the one you told me last night. She must have thought I meant it. She tossed a skillet at my head and flew out of here.'

'I shouldn't wonder,' he said. 'These people take such things pretty seriously.' He started toward the door. Gaye moved as though to go with him, but he stopped her. 'No, you stay here, I'll handle it.'

He was gone for nearly an hour. Finally she heard him come in the front way and hurried out into the hall to meet him.

'Is she all right?' she asked.

'Yes, I took her home and told her to take the day off,' he said. 'It took a while to get her calmed down, but I think she'll be back tomorrow.'

'I'm sorry,' Gaye said. 'I forget how seriously some people take these things. And I didn't even know anyone would hear me, I was only thinking aloud.'

'That can be very dangerous when you're thinking about something so frightening.' He spoke sharply and she could see that he was annoyed.

'Carlton, is there really a *loukerouk*?' The words came from her so spontaneously she had no time to contemplate them. She had not consciously meant to ask that question, but there it was, and suddenly she was glad to have it out.

For a long time, Carlton said nothing. He was fighting with his own conscience. At last the truth came out of him in one clipped word.

'Yes,' he said.

She did not try to detain him with more questions. Certainly there were many that she wanted to ask, now that she had opened that Pandora's box, but she knew that she was not yet ready to deal with some of them.

Dinner was not the pleasant affair that evening that it had been for the past few days. Carlton was withdrawn and she wondered if he regretted his admission to her. Perhaps, she thought, despite his confession, he did not really believe in such things. It might be that he felt foolish.

'I feel so restless,' Susan complained later in the evening, when Gaye had gone to sit with her. Susan was out of bed at the time, standing at her window. 'It's the full moon, I suppose.'

Gaye shuddered. 'Why do you say that?' Had Louise talked to her of the *loukerouk* too?

Susan only shrugged. 'They say the full moon makes people restless, or something like that. What did the doctor say about our leaving?'

'A few more days.' If only, she thought, it could be right now, at once. If they could only escape from the spell of this place, where unreal things seemed real and fear was always at your side.

She had one thing to be grateful for. Susan seemed much less despondent than she had been. It might almost have been that she accepted what had happened to her as just punishment for her past behaviour. At least she had made no further comments upon her scars, nor did she complain about the Crays and the fortune that had slipped through her fingers. Whether this was tact or a change of heart, Gaye did not know, but she chose not to push her luck by bringing the subject up.

She finished the coffee she had brought with her. The cup rattled on the saucer.

Her hands were not as steady as they ought to be.

'You know, I think the moon's gotten to you, too,' Susan said.

'I suppose that must be it,' Gaye said with a smile, but she grew sober when she was ready to leave. Be it the moon or what have you, she *did* feel apprehensive. All the talk of werewolves and full moons and spells and charms had not settled well with her.

'Do me a favour,' she said at the door. 'Lock your door for tonight, will you?'

'Why?'

'Just because I do feel nervous, and I'll feel better if I know your door is locked.'

Susan gave another shrug. 'If you like,' she said.

Gaye waited outside until she heard the click of the lock. In her own room she was careful to see that the bolts were on as well.

She had no sooner gotten into bed when there was a knock at her door. 'Who's there?' she asked, annoyed to realize that her voice sounded so frightened.

'It's Carlton,' came the reply. 'Don't be alarmed, I just want to talk to you for a minute.'

She slipped on a robe and turned on the lights before letting him in. To her surprise, he had a gun in his hand, a small pistol. He gave it to her.

'Do I need this?' she asked, holding it gingerly. In the middle of the woods, knowing that Susan had just been attacked, it had seemed reasonable to have a gun in her hand, but surely it was unnecessary here.

'I hope not,' he said, 'but I want you to have it just in case. And I want you to make me a promise. If you feel yourself in any danger, from any source, I want you to use that gun.'

He was so serious in manner and tone of voice that she could not joke about it, nor question his wishes. 'All right,' she said.

But he seemed not quite satisfied to leave it at that. 'You must understand,' he said, 'you are to use it to protect yourself, no matter against whom. Do you get that?'

'But, who do you think . . . ?'

He interrupted her with a shake of his head. 'Anybody. Even against me if you think you're in any danger from me. Will you promise me that, to use it no matter who is threatening you?'

She tried to understand what was in his eyes. 'But I couldn't,' she said, 'not if it were you.'

The ghost of a smile played upon his lips. Then, quite unexpectedly, he seized her in his arms. Before she half knew what was happening, he was kissing her. Her heart seemed to burst into song. She forgot death and tragedy, werewolves and charms and spirits and everything unpleasant. There was nothing to the world except those strong arms crushing her to him, and those lips upon hers.

It ended too soon, but she would have thought that if it had lasted a lifetime. He stepped back from her, looking as flushed as she felt, and his breath was rapid and uneven.

'Carlton.' His name was like music on her lips. 'I love you,' she said.

'I fell in love with you from the first

moment I saw you,' he said. She would have come to him again, but he raised a hand to restrain her. 'I only hope our love is strong enough for what may happen.'

She felt tears welling up in her eyes. She could not bear the thought that anything might spoil their love.

'What could happen?' she asked plaintively. 'Tell me, please.'

He shook his head forlornly. 'No, no, I can't do that. Only, for my sake, please, protect yourself with that gun, I beg you.'

Before she could argue, he was gone, slipping quietly from her room. She wanted to run after him and beg him for all the truth, but she knew he did not want that. He had asked her to have faith in him, and she must.

She sat on the edge of the bed, staring at the gun. A thought came to her and she broke the gun open, taking out one of the bullets. It was fashioned of silver. She found herself wondering if it had been blessed by Saint Hubert.

When she went back to bed, however, the gun was tucked safely between the mattress and the springs, where she could reach it with a single movement of her hand. She fell asleep feeling safe and loved.

She woke frightened. Once again the howling of a wolf carried across the night air. She sat up, fumbling for a light. The howl came again. She shivered and pulled the blanket up about her shoulders.

The silence that followed seemed interminable. She could only guess at its length, and she had no great confidence in her guesses. It might have been five minutes, or twenty. At last it seemed that it was finished for the night.

She was about to turn out her light, when she thought of Susan. Knowing her sister, Susan would be frightened out of her wits.

I'd better go look in on her, Gaye thought. She got out of bed and once more slipped on her robe. She was almost to her door when she heard a sound in the hall. Her first thought was that it was Susan, and she almost called out.

Something about the sound stopped her, though. It sounded somehow stealthy and furtive. She remained silent, staring at the door. No one called her name. If it were Susan, she would certainly have called by now.

Then, as she watched, the knob turned slowly. Gaye stared in horrified fascination. The door was not locked by key and the latch clicked, but the bolt held the door firmly in place.

The knob turned back. There was silence. Gaye stepped backward as quietly as she could, until she had reached the side of her bed. She felt for the gun and brought it out.

It was several minutes before she could bring herself to open the door. When she had slipped the bolt, deliberately being noisy, she stepped back a few feet to see if anyone would burst into the room. She had the gun raised, the safety off, ready to shoot.

No one did, and finally she had to go back to the door and, heart in throat, tug it open. There was no one waiting on the other side, and no one in sight in the hall.

To get to Susan's room, she would have to walk this entire hall, and the central hall, mount the main stairs and follow almost the same route in the floor above — but she had to know if Susan was safe.

Carefully she closed her door after herself. The latch click sounded like a pistol shot. Even her breath was loud in the dark hall. She moved as quickly and as noiselessly as she could, looking from right to left at every doorway. When she reached the stairs, she fairly flew up them, but at the top she again moved with caution.

Susan's door was still safely locked. She rapped softly.

'Who's there?' Susan demanded from within.

'It's Gaye, let me in.'

In a minute the door was open. Gaye slipped inside and locked it again at once.

'Good grief, what are you doing with that gun?' Susan asked, looking bewildered.

Gaye did not want to mention any mysterious prowlers. 'All that racket,' she said, 'I thought you might be frightened.'

'All what racket? I didn't hear a thing,' Susan said.

14

Although she did not explain her reasons for doing so, Gaye spent the night in Susan's room. Nothing further happened. It occurred to her that Carlton might come to look in on her and be alarmed by her absence, but she quickly decided that he was bright enough to come here first, to see if she were with Susan.

Susan had returned to sleep at once, aided by the mild sedative she had taken since the attack. It was not much later before Gaye fell into her own troubled sleep. Nightmares of strange dark beasts left her nearly as tired when she woke as though she had not slept at all.

Carlton did come in the morning, quite early. He tapped at the door and called her name. 'Yes, I'll be right there,' she called back.

'No, it isn't necessary, I only wanted to be sure you were all right.' Then he was gone.

When Gaye came down to breakfast, it was with a new resolve in her heart. She had felt for some days as if she were a house divided against itself. She knew that she loved Carlton, but despite that love, she could not entirely put aside her suspicions. She wanted to trust him, but too many strange incidents suggested that he was not altogether innocent in the tragic events that had taken place.

In a few days, perhaps even the following day, she would be leaving Craywood. Away from Carlton, she could better face her feelings and deal with them, but before she could make any sort of decisions, she had to uncover the truth. No matter how painful it was, she had to know what secrets Carlton was hiding. Whatever he knew about the murders that had occurred — even if he himself were that murderer — she wanted to know. And much as she wanted to dismiss even that last grim possibility, she could not. He was a man unlike any other she had known. Loving him was not understanding him.

As to the *loukerouk*, she did not pretend even to herself to understand what that was all about. She could not imagine that werewolves existed, but something, man or beast, had killed here, and if it were a man, there were pitifully few possibilities. A woman could not have committed the atrocities that had been committed, and surely Dennis, confined to his wheelchair, could not roam the forests, spring upon unsuspecting people, and kill. Stoddard had the necessary strength and agility, but his own fear was convincing.

Of course, it need not be someone from Craywood at all, but that suggested a dubious coincidence in that all of the horrible deaths had occurred here. Or, it might be, as apparently others believed, that there really was a wild animal of some sort in the woods — but no trace had ever been found except for those puzzling wolf hairs the Sheriff had uncovered.

Could Carlton, the man she loved, be a murderer? On the face of it, that almost seemed the only sensible answer — unless, of course, one granted the existed of a *loukerouk*. Or perhaps Walter's forest demon, Pan?

She had mulled over all these questions before. What was changed now was that she had resolved to answer them. She knew that it would do no good to ask Carlton directly. She had tried, but she knew that he would not yet give her explanations, for whatever reason of his own.

She would have to ferret out the truth herself, and she meant to do so as soon as she was able. She planned to begin with a search of Carlton's rooms. Surely if he were guilty, there would be some clue there. It went against the grain, to stoop to such underhanded methods, but he had given her no other alternative, and she had to believe that in this instance, the end justified the means.

Just how she could search Carlton's room without his knowledge, she did not know, but he himself gave her the opportunity that very evening. When dinner was finished, he announced that he was going to closet himself in the library downstairs, straightening out some complicated legal papers.

'I expect I'll work late,' he said, 'so I'll

bid you good night now. And, again, I caution you to protect yourself.'

She waited until he had been in the library long enough to be settled to his work. Then, subduing her guilt feelings, Gaye stole up the stairs to his rooms.

She was overcome by a wave of emotion as she stood in his sitting room. It reflected him so thoroughly that the room seemed permeated with his presence. All of the love she felt for him weighed upon her like a great burden. She felt apprehensive about what she might find here. What would she do if she learned the worst?

I must face that when it comes, she told herself firmly, squaring her shoulders. Whatever she learned would be better than the nagging suspicions and uncertainties that plagued her now.

Searching a man's room was a new experience for her. It was made doubly awkward by the fact that she did not even know for what she was searching. She went to the door that led to his bedroom, but that surely was the least likely of the two rooms, and she gave her attention to his sitting room instead.

Her eyes lighted on the desk, its surface littered with papers and books. Certainly that would be a logical place to begin. She went to it and lighted the desk lamp and seated herself in the big old chair behind the desk.

Again guilt assailed her as she picked up a large folder of papers that were most likely to be personal. Reluctant to read them, she let her eyes range over the desktop, and saw the title on a book jacket. Its large letters immediately caught her eye: *Beasts of the Night*.

She set the folder aside and picked up the book, turning it over. It fell open of its own accord, as though it had been opened often to this same spot. The page that lay before her was the beginning page of a chapter dealing with werewolves.

She looked at another of the books on the desk top. That entire volume was on the subject of werewolves, as were the other two books on the desk. One of them called the subject lycanthropy, but when she turned to its beginning page she learned that the word was a technical term for werewolfism.

'Lycanthropy, or *morbus lupinus*, as it is called,' she read, 'can be classified as an uncommon type of encephalitis, an acute infectious encephalitis, and not a form of monomania. It is the condition known to laymen as werewolfism.'

She put the book aside. This was how Carlton knew so much about the *loukerouk*. Those evenings when he had allegedly been working on the affairs of the estate, he had instead been studying up on the werewolf — the lycanthrope.

Again she picked up the folder that had first caught her eye, and opened it. It was a collection of notes. She recognized Carlton's handwriting, and it came to her that this was his 'homework,' the pertinent information he had gleaned from the various reference books.

Attached to the inside of the folder with a paper clip was a receipt. She removed it and read it. It was from a mail order firm that called itself Safari Imports, and specialized in the bizarre and sporty gift, according to its motto. It was made out to Carlton Cray, and the receipt was for one Arctic wolf skin, shipped post-paid.

For a moment she closed her eyes and fought back a sob that rose in her throat. She remembered at once the grisly ceremony Carlton had described to her, the ritual for becoming a werewolf. It required donning a wolf skin.

She forced herself to take up the notes in the folder, leaning toward the light to read them more easily. She had come here to learn the truth. She must not shrink from it now.

The notes were informal, as though Carlton had been trying to sort out his own thoughts on the paper. Some of them were obviously copied word for word from the various texts. Others appeared to be thoughts of his own that had occurred to him as he read.

'Lycanthrope — werewolf,' followed by a list of synonyms. Some of them Gaye remembered from Carlton's description. *Loukerouk* was there, and its original form, *loupgarou*.

'A form of paranoia,' she read. 'The lycanthrope feels hunted. Set off by strong emotion, either sudden, or long standing. Hate, for instance, of a brother.' The latter phrase was underlined. 'According to legend, the loup-garou is a sorcerer who, in the guise of a wolf, runs in the fields at night. His skin is proof against a bullet unless it has been blessed in a chapel of Saint Hubert.'

She sat for a moment, thinking. What she was reading about was not the werewolfism of old movies and grim tales. This was a medical fact, a mental condition. This she could not laugh off as an old witch's tale. She no longer had to think she was dealing with the supernatural, but somehow that fact made the subject all the more chilling.

She read on, comprehension taking shape in her mind. A note marked, 'Verstegan, 1625,' read: ' . . . not onely unto the view of others seem as wolves, but to their owne thinking have both the shape and nature of wolves.' Another, annotated, 'Encyl. Brit.,' read: ' . . . pathological condition manifesting a depraved appetite and an irresistible desire for raw flesh, often that of human beings . . .'

There came to her mind a picture of Walter as she had seen him dead. One arm had been severed completely. She had never asked what had happened to it.

'Oh, my God,' she whispered aloud as she grasped the implications of what she had seen and read.

She suddenly remembered the conversation she had overheard between Walter and Carlton. 'You don't know what it's like,' Carlton had told his brother, 'To be in the grip of a horror like this, to be controlled by it as though you had no will of your own.'

Controlled by it . . . an irresistible desire . . . they were the same thing, weren't they?

There was an account of a French family, the Danillons of St. Claude, all of whom confessed to being werewolves in 1598 and were put to their deaths.

Lycanthropy was again and again described as a disease. It was common to mental defectives, although apparently not limited to them. The sufferer was sometimes convinced that he actually was a wild animal. He might crave raw meat, run on all fours, even howl like a wolf.

How many nights had she heard that horrible shrieking, so like a wolf and yet not exactly that either — a person mocking a wolf, although she had not guessed that at the time?

'The disease may give the victim the delusion that he has been physically transformed. Lycanthropes often insist, despite witnesses to the contrary, that they have assumed the shape of a wolf.

'When the afflicted sinks his teeth in,' read a note from the *Journal de psychologie normale et pathologique*, Paris, 1907, 'He is filled by a great satisfaction.'

A lengthy quote from the *Dictionaire encyclopédique des sciences médicales* described four forms of lycanthropy. In the first of these, the victim suffered delusion combined with guilt mania. He withdrew, often isolating himself, and falsely laid claim to running the forests at night, killing and other bizarre acts. Commonly he would beg to be put to death, usually in some awful way, such as burning at the stake.

The second form of lycanthrope had essentially the same delusions but, if permitted, would go so far as to roam the woods at night and even howl and scream, but physically they were harmless.

In the third category were placed those who suffered hallucinations due to drugs such as belladonna, henbane, and Jimson weed. Here Carlton had added a penciled question: LSD?

The fourth group was the most grisly. It told of the lycanthropes who suffered true werewolfism. With the coming of night, or sometimes deluding themselves that it was night when it was not, they would begin to feel uneasy. This would grow, until they were no longer in control of themselves. Sometimes they would be unconscious of their acts, and would waken the following day with no recollection of what had transpired.

Under the influence of their seizure, they would go from their homes, roaming forests and fields. They would attack animals, even people. They might continue this for a night or for days at a time.

Their clothes rotted away or might be removed in a fit. Hair and beard grow long. In some cases, the facial characteristics seemed to undergo physical change, and the fingernails to become longer and coarser. They were soiled with filth and with blood, their hair matted, until they had taken on the physical appearance of the legendary werewolf.

There were notes on cures. White hellebore had once been thought a cure, but was no longer regarded as of any value. Folk cures were numerous: apples, fresh eggs morning and night, various herbs. The lycanthrope could be warded off with clear water, burning sulphur, fire, silver bullets, violet root, wolfsbane, rye, mistletoe, ash, and yew trees.

Other notes told traditional ways of recognizing the werewolf: straight slanting eyebrows that met over the nose were considered a certain sign. A long third finger on each hand was another, as were curved and reddish looking fingernails, and small ears set low on the head.

There were many more historical cases of lycanthropy and more folklore, but

Gaye had learned enough. She closed the folder and sat staring before her, thinking of what she had read.

It seemed almost certain that Carlton was a lycanthrope. It was the only explanation that fitted the facts. Only one thing softened the shock — according to what she had read, the lycanthrope might not be conscious of his actions.

She could see how it must have been. At first, Carlton might have been completely unaware of what he was doing. Then, something aroused his suspicions. Perhaps he had found blood on his clothing. Puzzled, he had begun to investigate the subject, more and more deeply. He had asked her for a little more time. He must have thought he could find some means to cure himself of the sickness.

Her eyes filled with tears. She thought of his long-standing resentment of Walter. It was that, no doubt, that had set him off, and what more logical victims than two girls who had once loved Walter, perhaps still did.

Then, as the truth dawned on him, that

agonizing confession to Walter, and eventually, when Walter tried to restrain him, the taking of Walter's life — and, of course, that vicious attack on Susan, he could hardly have prevented himself from that. She shuddered to think that only her timely arrival had saved Susan's life.

It was horrible, but at least his actions had been unconscious. He had truly not been responsible for them. No court would execute him. He would be put away, but he would live, and time might yet offer a cure.

The thought of his imprisonment stirred her to action. She loved Carlton still, perhaps more than ever before, and she would stand by him, through whatever befell him, but she could not shield him. Though they were the acts of a man not in control of his mind, still his acts had been horrible, bestial in the worst sense of that word. Though it broke her heart, she must see that he was taken into custody.

What was she to do, though? Should she risk talking to Carlton? Ordinarily he was lucid and receptive to her ideas.

Perhaps knowing her love and knowing she would remain loyal to him, he would be willing to surrender to the authorities.

What if he did not? Her knowledge would necessitate his fleeing, in that case. He might kill again. The thought flashed through her mind that he might kill her, but that, she dismissed at once. He had had opportunities to do that before. She was not afraid of Carlton. He loved her and she was certain that love would protect her, but some innocent person might suffer in her place. Dared she take that chance, risk another death? Or ought she to go to the authorities, to Sheriff Lester, with what she knew?

Would he even believe her? It was an incredible tale, documented though it was with medical evidence, and though he was no doubt a sincere and dedicated man, the Sheriff hardly possessed a sophisticated knowledge of psychiatrics.

She determined to take the folder with her. If he read the material as she had just done, he could hardly fail to give some credence to what it contained. The essential thing was that he realize Carlton was ill and must be treated accordingly.

'Oh, Carlton,' she prayed silently, 'Forgive me, darling.'

She took the folder and started from the room, but she got no further than the door. Even as she reached for it, the door opened and Carlton stood before her.

He looked at her in surprise and then his eyes darted at once to his desk. When they came back to her, they rested on the folder in her hands.

15

It was an awful moment. Gaye could not follow all the emotions that went across Carlton's face as he stared at her. Anger, fear, sadness, disappointment. If ever she had hoped that the ground could open and swallow her up, it was now.

'Carlton, I . . . ' she began finally.

'Have you read that?' he interrupted her, indicating the folder.

'Yes.' A sob caught in her throat. 'Oh, darling, I know now, but I love you anyway, do you understand that? I'll stand by you no matter what happens. You must have faith in me.'

She spoke all in a rush, her words running together. She must make him trust her, she must!

For a moment he continued to stare at her. He had a puzzled look as though a piece that he knew fitted into a puzzle would not go into place. Then, suddenly, comprehension lighted up his features.

He grabbed her fiercely, pulling her close.

'*What* do you know?' he asked hoarsely.

'Carlton, I swear it . . . '

'No, tell me, what do you know? Put it into words,' he demanded.

She could scarcely see him for the tears that filled her eyes. His rough grip was hurting her arm but she was only dimly aware of the pain. 'I know that you killed those people, Walter and those girls,' she sobbed, 'but I know that you couldn't help it, that you had no control over it.'

He held her like that for what seemed an eternity, and through the haze of her tears she saw the horror on his face.

'My God,' he said at last. Then, so abruptly that she nearly lost her balance, he released her and turned from her. She heard him running down the hall.

'Carlton, wait,' she cried, running after him, but before she could reach him he was out of the house and the engine of his car roared to life. The tires squealed as he sped away from Craywood, driving with all the speed at his command.

She stood for a moment at the door, sobbing and staring after him, but as the first shock wave of hysteria passed, she began to think again.

'What must I do?' she asked herself anxiously. The answer was, that depended upon what Carlton would do. He was in a state of anger and disappointment. Memory of the notes she had read flashed through her mind. Strong emotion set the lycanthrope off. Because of her, Carlton might kill again, tonight.

Close on the heels of that thought came another. All the deaths had centred around Craywood. If he were going to kill, it would be here, and though she wanted to believe that his love for her would protect her, she could not believe Craywood was safe. Dennis was his own brother, but so had Walter been, and he hated Susan. He had tried once before to kill her, and he might very well choose to finish the job.

She had an urge to go after Carlton, but her Chevy would never catch his Ferrari, and anyway he had too long a start on her. No, what she had to do first was get Dennis and Susan to safety. Carlton would return, she was sure of it, and when he did so, he might not be in control of his actions.

She ran the length of the house for her car keys and the gun Carlton had given her. Her Chevy was in the garage. She decided to bring it to the front door so she would have only a few feet to assist Susan and Dennis.

The car would not start, however. It had not been driven for several days now and the battery was too low. The grinding of the starter followed a descending pitch, and finally ceased altogether.

The family Caddy was parked beside the Chevy. She went to it and looked in, hoping, but the keys were not in it. She pushed back a lock of hair and tried to think back. Stoddard had gotten the keys from Carlton the day of Walter's funeral, but where had Carlton gotten them from?

She ran into the house again, to the den, and found the keys in the desk there, and ran back to the garage. The big sedan sprang to life at once. She backed it around and pulled up to the front steps of the house, leaving the motor running while she went for Dennis and Susan.

Dennis seemed more than a little surprised to see her. He was reading. In the fireplace a bright fire had the room uncomfortably warm.

'Say, you look like you've seen a ghost,' he said when she came in.

'I think I have,' she said. 'Look, we've got to leave Craywood, right away. Get yourself ready, will you, while I go for Susan.'

'Leave Craywood?' He looked bewildered. 'You must be joking. What on earth for?'

She shook her head. 'I haven't time to explain it all now. But I know about the wolf, and I've got to get you away from here before . . . before it's too late.'

He turned pale. 'You know?' he asked softly. 'About the deaths — and everything?'

'Yes, yes.' She was almost crying again from impatience. Time was speeding by. At any minute Carlton might return. 'Oh, please, hurry, I've got to get Susan ready.'

'Where's Carlton?'

'He's out. Oh, Dennis . . . '

'Does he know that you know everything?' He had not moved at all, but his expression was anxious.

'Yes, don't you understand? That's why I've got to get you out of here before he comes back. I know you're his brother, but that didn't protect Walter, and Carlton is very angry, and anger . . . oh, there isn't time, I'll explain everything in the car.'

'I see.' He appeared to be digesting what she had told him. 'Yes. I understand.'

'I'll come back for you in a minute,' she said. 'I have to get Susan to the car.'

She gave him no further opportunity for question, and hurried instead to Susan's room. Susan was in bed, reading. Her first pleasant greeting turned to one of concern as she saw Gaye's anxiety.

'Hello — oh, something's wrong.'

'There isn't time to explain just now,' Gaye said, rummaging in the closet for a coat. 'We've got to get away from here right now, it's not safe.'

Susan clambered from her bed, her eyes wide. 'Good Heavens, what is it, what's happened?'

Gaye thrust a coat at her. 'I'll tell you

all about it when we're safely away. Here, put this on. Shoes?'

'On the rack.' Susan put her questions aside and slipped hurriedly into the coat, buttoning it over her nightgown. Gaye took her arm to support her and, as quickly as Susan was able, they went along the hall and down the stairs.

There was still no sign of Carlton. Gaye helped Susan into the car. 'I've got to get Dennis,' she said.

'My God, you aren't going to leave me here alone,' Susan demanded.

The gun was on the seat of the car. Gaye handed it to her. 'Here. And keep the door locked.'

Her chest ached from the running she had done already, but fear gave her the strength to race to Dennis' room. The front room of his apartment was empty. She thought he must have gone into his bedroom to change.

Then she saw his chair, sitting empty across the room, and a chill went through her. Could something have happened? Could Carlton have come back already, entering the house through another door?

'Dennis?' she called. There was no answer. Across the room, the door to his bedroom stood open, the room beyond it dark. She called his name again and crossed to the bedroom door. When there was still no answer, she stepped through it.

In the pale light from behind her she saw an animal skin hanging from a peg on the door. She looked at it curiously. It was bluish grey, and she thought at once of wolves. She reached a tentative hand out to touch it. The hair was long and coarse. Slowly she turned one corner of it back. She could just make out the trade name stamped there: Safari Imports.

A wolf skin, the wolf skin that Carlton had purchased. Had it been a gift for Dennis, or had Dennis, in fact, ordered it himself, using Carlton's name? And if that were so . . . ?

There was hardly time for the grim significance of her discover to seep into her consciousness. A sound, low and muted, that might have been a snarl, brought her head up. Dennis was across the room from her. He had been in the shadows where, her eyes unused to the dark, she had not seen him. Now he had moved out into the dim light, crouching.

At first, she thought he looked like he was about to leap at her, but then she realized it was just the way he was standing. Only then did the full truth come to her — he was standing!

She stared at the thin twisted limbs that had always been hidden beneath blankets. They were grotesque, bent like some bizarre pair of parentheses. His feet were tiny shriveled objects that seemed to be turned on their sides. As he moved slowly toward her, shuffling along in a pathetic gait, she stared at those feet, imagining the tracks they would make. She had seen those tracks, beyond her terrace, and about Walter's body.

She forced herself at last to look into his face. Never before had she seen naked evil, but she knew she was looking upon it now. His eyes seemed to have turned red in the reflected light. His hair, normally combed so neatly, was tousled so that it lay about his head like the mane of an animal. His mouth was distorted into a horrible grimace, and from its corner ran a stream of spittle. To her fear-crazed senses his teeth seemed to have grown fanglike.

Her limbs refused to respond. She shook her head in disbelief as he came slowly toward her. 'Oh, no,' she managed to gasp. 'Oh, no!'

She came to her senses at last. She whirled about and dashed into the front room, racing wildly for the door. She had thought his twisted limbs would have made him slow, but he moved with incredible speed. She ducked to avoid a hand flung out to seize her, and veered from her path, but that let him reach the door before her. He slammed it violently shut and stood in front of it, grinning horribly at her.

She backed slowly away from him, her mind whirling. The French windows were behind her. If she could only reach them, get one open . . .

She darted in that direction but again he was too quick. She circled a chair, flinging it in his path to slow him, but he caught her arm in his fingers. She jerked away, but fell against another chair and this time she slipped, falling to the floor.

In an instant he was on her. In terror she struggled against his strong grip, kicking and writhing. His lips were pulled back from his teeth. He lowered his face toward her and she knew that he meant to tear open her throat with those teeth. She screamed in horror and threw herself aside. His teeth scraped her flesh, bringing blood. She knew he had only to close them upon her throat and he would end her life.

She kicked out with all her strength. The table beside them toppled. The brass lamp upon it fell heavily on his shoulder, breaking his hold on her, and he roared with pain.

In that second she was able to break free. She scrambled away, but fingers of steel grabbed her ankle. Then, as hope faded within her, her eyes fell upon the fireplace, with its flames still dancing behind the mesh screen.

She knocked the screen aside. Hot ash burned her hand, and her attacker realized her intention, but her fingers closed around a burning log and before he could stop her she had it in her hand.

He shrieked in anger and fear and let her go, jumping to his feet. Gasping for breath, she held the torch between them and got to her knees. If she could reach the door . . . she glanced in that direction and with a roar he darted toward her, trying to seize the burning log. She struck him with it, thrusting it into his face. The smell of burning hair mingled with his screams and his shirt began to smoulder

Screaming in terror, he ran around in a circle, slapping at the smoking fabric and trying to rip it from his body. Gaye scrambled to her feet and ran for the door, but he saw her and came after her. Again she struck out at him with her fiery weapon, thrusting it at his face and forcing him back, but she knew if she turned to open the door, he would be upon her again, and she could not hold him off like this forever.

Then, miraculously, she heard her name called. It was Carlton. He was back.

'Carlton,' she screamed. 'Here, in Dennis's room.'

She saw that even in his crazed condition the monster understood. He looked from her to the door behind him. In his eyes was raw hatred. He made a final move toward her. The torch stopped him and suddenly he turned and rushed away, toward the windows. He crashed into them. Glass showered the room. The flimsy molding gave and he was through and disappearing into the darkness beyond even as the door behind her crashed open.

Then, mercifully she was in Carlton's arms, sobbing against his chest.

16

'Susan, she's outside,' she gasped, remembering her sister waiting in the car.

'She's all right,' he said, holding her close. 'She was about to shoot me when you screamed. Good Lord, you're bleeding. Here, let me see.'

He got her into a chair and examined the wound at her throat. 'Not too deep, thank God,' he said. 'I'll get something to put on it.'

'Carlton.' She grabbed his sleeve to hold him there. 'It was Dennis. I thought . . . '

'Not now,' he said, 'We'll talk about it in a little while, okay?' He left and came back with towels and bandages. She leaned back wearily in the chair and let him tend to her.

'That'll hold the bleeding,' he said after a moment. 'I'll get your sister to take care of you, all right?'

She closed her eyes. Despite all she had been through, despite the horror of the last few minutes, there was a sense of elation within her. She had been wrong, insanely, stupidly wrong. Carlton was not a murderer.

'Let him forgive me, please,' she prayed silently.

Susan was there in a minute. 'Where's Carlton?' Gaye demanded when she saw her sister alone. 'He hasn't gone after . . . ?

'No,' Susan reassured her, pushing her back into the chair. 'He's phoning the Sheriff. He said you'd been hurt. Oh, dear.' She leaned down to examine the cut.

'It's not bad, really, it's stopped bleeding already.'

Susan dressed the wound neatly and brought Gaye a brandy. Carlton returned in a few minutes.

'The Sheriff will be here shortly with all the men he can round up.' He saw the question in Gaye's eyes and added, 'I told him the truth this time.'

He gave Susan a searching look. 'You must be about done in yourself.'

'I am.' She was showing the effects of so much effort after her convalescence.

'But I can hold out if I'm needed.'

'No, it'll be all right now. I'll stay with Gaye until the boys get here. Want me to help you upstairs?'

She gave him a funny look. She had been on unfriendly terms with him so long, it was odd for them to be so considerate of one another now. 'No, I'll be all right,' she told him. 'And I do think I need to lie down. But let me know what happens, okay?'

'I think we'll be more comfortable in the den,' Carlton said to Gaye when they were alone. 'And I can keep that room locked until the Sheriff gets here, just in case.'

In the den, he locked the doors and windows, and poured them both drinks. 'I think you need this,' he said, handing her a glass.

'Carlton,' she said finally, 'can you ever forgive me for thinking it was you?'

'I already have,' he said. She knew from his voice and his expression that the pain was still with him, but there was sincerity in his forgiveness too. In time, the wound would heal.

'There isn't much else you could have thought, under the circumstances,' he said. 'I was hurt and angry when I took off out of here, but even as I drove, I thought back over everything, seeing it as it must have looked to you, and I realized you weren't to blame for what you thought. And, of course, as soon as I had calmed down, I realized what sort of danger I had left you in, and I came straight back.

'I should ask you to forgive me. I should have told you everything long ago, but all I had were suspicions for most of the time, and even though the truth was staring me in the face, well, it's a hard thing to believe about your own brother. I thought it was impossible, that I must be crazy even to imagine it. I had never seen him out of his chair except when he was in bed, or someone was carrying him. I had no idea . . . '

'I understand,' she said softly. 'Who could have dreamed?' He took her hand and squeezed it.

He paused, not so much as if he were reluctant to speak, but rather as though he were sorting out his thoughts, trying to decide where to begin.

'I don't understand all of it exactly,' he said. 'I'm no psychiatrist, or even a doctor. As nearly as I could put together, it's a type of insanity. Paranoia, they call it, and God knows, poor Dennis had reason enough to become paranoid — crippled the way he was, shut up in this awful old house. Walter loathed him. Oh, he never said so in so many words. I don't suppose he even fully realized it himself, but he loathed what Dennis was.'

'He never spoke of him to me,' Gaye said. 'In the past, when I knew him.'

'No, he wouldn't. And Dennis was smart enough to realize how Walter felt. Dennis and I got along all right, but the truth is, I was hardly ever here. If I had been, things might have been different.'

'You can't blame yourself.'

He gave her a grateful smile. 'I didn't even know he had learned to walk. That was a secret between him and the Stoddards. I guess he was afraid Walter would laugh at him because he was so ungraceful, hobbling around the way he did, so he kept it to himself all these years.

'He was just a little kid when our parents died. The Stoddards practically raised him. They were the closest to him. Louise was like a mother. She would sit here of an evening and entertain him with stories of the bayou. Of course, they were all about witches and vampires and ghosts — and werewolves. And Dennis was fascinated by them. Whenever he asked me for books, it was always something along those lines. And he asked me to buy him a wolf skin as a present. I thought it was an odd gift, but I couldn't refuse him. That's what comes of feeling guilty for neglecting somebody. You give in to their requests without questioning them.

'Somewhere he had gotten the idea of becoming a werewolf, maybe because it represented power to him. Louise had told him the legends of the rituals you had to go through, and I suppose maybe he was already suffering the milder stages of lycanthropy. He thought he needed the wolf skin to undergo the transformation. Apparently he went through the entire ritual, with or without the Stoddards' help. After that, as near as I can put together, whenever he went through these spells, he believed he was in the shape of a wolf.'

Carlton paused to sip his drink reflectively. Gaye did not prompt him to hurry. She knew that all of this was painful for him, but she realized too what a relief it must be to unburden himself of the great weight he had carried all this time.

'I suppose,' he went on after a moment, 'that at first he did not remember what all he had done. I'm sure of it. That's one of the things that so confused me, in fact. I asked him about it, and he knew nothing about the deaths of those girls. I was convinced I could tell when Dennis was lying or telling the truth, so I believed him — but of course, he wasn't actually lying, he really did not consciously know what he had done, not until a little later.

'I think it just built up all these years. The hatred for Walter, the belief in his were-wolfism, and eventually, that hatred spreading to anything Walter loved or that loved Walter. I don't know exactly how those girls got into it. I suppose chance remarks stayed on in his mind until they took on an undue importance.

'When he killed the first one — he may simply have stumbled on her accidentally while he was roaming the forest — the Stoddards, of course, became suspicious. Stoddard started following him when he would steal out at night. The night he killed that second girl, Stoddard came along too late to save the girl, but in time to know what had happened.

'He and his wife were scared out of their wits, but Dennis scared them even more. He told them if they talked to anyone about this, he would bring them into it as his accomplices. They kept their silence, but that's when they stopped working here at night, and started protecting themselves with every kind of charm Louise could think up.'

Gaye thought of the silver ornament Louise had given her and the repeated warnings about the *loukerouk*. 'She really tried to save me,' she said. A sudden thought occurred to her. 'Carlton, you said that charm she gave me might actually save my life. And you told me that day in the woods to go into the creek.'

'You're forgetting the all important element. Dennis didn't turn into a werewolf, in the sense of those old monster films. He *thought* he turned into a wolf, and because he believed all those old legends, he would have been afraid of the silver or the Devil's dung, and afraid to step into running water. He would have believed those things could repel him, and so they might have done just that.'

'I see.'

'I was here at the time of that second murder. There were already rumours about wolves, and when I looked at the body, I too found some loose hairs. I took them into San Francisco myself to have them checked. When I found out they were wolf hairs, I started to get suspicious.

'That's when I talked to Dennis. He convinced me of his innocence, but the talk inevitably turned to werewolves, and

I began to look into the subject more thoroughly. Of course, that brought me to the subject of lycanthropy. And by this time, you had arrived.'

'Susan called me because she was frightened. She thought it was Walter killing people.' Gaye remembered her drive to Craywood. 'Oh, that night, when I had the accident, I hit someone, it must have been Dennis. He dashed in front of my car, but I only grazed him, I think. He got up and vanished into the forest. I went after him to try to help him, but he just disappeared.'

'It probably was him. It wasn't until well after we arrived at the house that he made an appearance. You mean you followed him into the forest?'

Gaye nodded and shivered. She had been in the darkness with an insane killer. 'Thank heaven you came along when you did.'

'Yes.' He thought for a moment. 'I had stopped my car a half a mile or so back along the road. I thought I heard howling, but it didn't come again, and I went on, until I saw your car. My first thought was that there had been another death. Then, when you came out of the darkness . . . I may as well tell you, you really scared me.' He smiled down at her.

'Me?' she said, surprised.

'There I was, a confirmed bachelor, who had vowed never to fall in love, let alone marry, and there you were, and I was in love with you at the very first sight.'

Gaye blushed but she was happy. She returned his kiss eagerly. He refreshed their drinks before going on.

'That first night, I thought I saw someone on your terrace. Susan wasn't the only one who suspected Walter. I had begun to wonder if he were up to something, so I dressed and went into the woods opposite your room, where I could keep an eye on you. I'd just met you, but already I was determined to see that nothing happened to you.'

'I saw you watching,' Gaye said. 'And to think, I thought you might have evil designs.'

'Most of the rest of it, I guess you can figure out for yourself. The more I read about lycanthropy, the more I began to suspect that Dennis was the killer, only, I still had no idea he could get around without his chair. That was why I couldn't bring myself to tell the Sheriff about it, I kept thinking he must be, and then I would decide he couldn't be. I talked to Walter about the disease, but he wouldn't believe it. He did say he would watch Dennis, so I settled down to keeping an eye on you.

'But, of course, I should have known better. With Dennis hating Walter as he did, and Walter not taking it seriously, the last thing I should have done was turn over to Walter the responsibility of keeping an eye on Dennis.

'You can imagine how I felt when Walter was killed, but I still had no proof, nothing but my own suspicions. And Dennis is my brother. I couldn't bear the thought of turning him over to the authorities until I was absolutely certain. Once I even suggested that he might have done those things, he would have been taken away and treated like an animal. I waited to be sure.'

He bent down to kiss her again. 'I was wrong in that, though. It was one thing to gamble with my own life, but another thing to gamble with yours. When your sister was attacked, I knew time was running out. The one thing that puzzled me was why Dennis didn't attack you, but even though he was in one of his spells, I think he must have remembered that you had tried to befriend him. He really did like you.'

'I thought that,' Gaye said. 'I think he would not have attacked me tonight, but I was suddenly a threat. He must have thought that I knew about him. I don't remember just what words I used with him, and I told him I meant to take him away from Craywood. That must have been an emotional wrench for him.'

'Yes. As much as he hated Craywood, it was the only home he had ever known. His lair, as it were.'

He paused and then began again. 'After Susan was attacked, I felt certain it had to be Dennis. I got hold of everything I could and really began to read about lycanthropy. That's what I was doing all those nights, studying in my room. I kept praying I'd find some genuine cure, but I didn't, and I had frankly made up my mind to throw in the towel. I had gotten all those notes together for the specific purpose of using them tomorrow. I meant to have Dennis committed. I was convinced that he was a killer, and insane, but I still didn't want to see him shot down like a beast, even though, for all practical purposes, that's about what he is now. That's what I was doing in the den, earlier this evening, making arrangements for him with a mental hospital. I thought if I could get him into an asylum, get doctors to commit him, I could tell the authorities the truth, knowing they couldn't do anything more to him.'

'You'd have succeeded, too, if I hadn't meddled,' Gaye said softly.

He hugged her closer. 'No, don't blame yourself. It was a selfish plan. I should have gone to the authorities long ago. I foolishly thought as long as I kept a close eye on him, nothing could happen, but I should have seen how easily that could slip up when he attacked Susan. I followed him to his room that day, and then I came after you, but all he had to do was go right out his windows and take the shorter route straight through the woods, and I never dreamed he could move as fast as he did. I still don't know whether he heard me coming, or thought he had managed to kill Susan, but it was a close call. I should have called things off right then.'

Lights played across the room as a car pulled up the drive, followed closely by two others. There was a sound of voices and the braying of dogs.

'That's the Sheriff,' Carlton said. 'You stay put. I'll be right back.'

He was gone for a few minutes. The voices of many men, arguing different points, calling to one another, exchanging jokes, drifted into the den. The dogs grew quiet for a time and then again erupted into excited noise.

Carlton came back. He had his gun strapped to his hips and carried a rifle besides. He also brought her pistol and handed it to her.

'Just in case,' he said. 'Although I don't

think there's any danger, not with all these men combing the woods. He knows we'll be after him, and he will probably just keep running, or maybe try to find someplace to hole up. We're bound to find him pretty quick, in any event.'

She saw the pain he was trying to conceal. She envisioned him racing through the forest, the dogs and braying, men shouting — and their prey was his own brother.

'You needn't go, you know,' she said, searching his eyes. 'They're bound to understand.'

'No, it's my place.' He kissed her lightly and then went out again to join the others. Gaye listened as their noises faded in the distance, disappearing into the woods that surrounded the house.

She put a pillow under her head, to protect her sore throat, and stretched out on the sofa. She shuddered to think of the pathetically sick creature they were after. She could not help pitying him. He was what he was through no fault of his own, and although he had tried to kill her earlier, she could not hate him.

She found herself hoping that somehow he might be taken alive, but even as she thought that, she knew it was not likely. This was no longer a man they were pursuing, it was a vicious animal. The men hunting him would not show mercy.

17

She woke with a start, surprised to discover that she had slept at all. Her watch told her she had been asleep nearly two hours. She felt stiff when she sat up, a combination of sleeping on the unfamiliar sofa and the struggle with Dennis earlier.

She felt a pang of guilt. She had meant to look in on Susan when Carlton left, to see that she was all right. She smoothed her skirt and went up the wide stairs, conscious as she went of the distant sound of the dogs. Perhaps they were coming back, she thought. Carlton would be home soon, and although what had happened would certainly sadden him, at least they would be together again, and their nightmare would be ended.

Susan was sound asleep. Gaye pulled a sheet up over her bare arms and gazed affectionately at her for a minute. Susan's narrow scrape with death had changed her. She was still sad, but she was no longer as cruel and bitter as she had been.

She put out the light and went to the window to pull the curtains aside. Moonlight flooded the room. It was the night of the full moon. The night, the tales would have it, when the *loukerouk* prowled.

Again she heard the braying of the dogs, sounding much closer now, clearly on their way back, their grim task accomplished. The *loukerouk*'s prowling was over forever, she thought sadly.

A movement below caught her eye. She stared down, trying to identify it. Nothing stirred. The scene below was of such innocent loveliness that one could scarcely imagine what horrors this place had fostered.

I must have imagined it, she thought, and started to turn from the window, but it came again, and this time she saw where it was. A shadow moved, separated itself from the other shadows, and moved across the lawn below.

Dennis! She saw him clearly as he crossed in the moonlight. Her hand went to her throat. She heard the dogs, coming ever closer, and understood in a flash what had happened. Dennis had managed so far to elude them. He had escaped them in the forest, circling about until he had come once again to Craywood. She did not have to guess why he had come back.

The back door was locked, she knew, she had checked it herself before leaving the kitchen, but the front door? Carlton had come and gone that way.

She ran from the room and down the hall, determined to get to the front door before Dennis did. If he were once inside the house, crazed as he was, she doubted that the flimsy door to Susan's room would keep him out, and even if it did, he would still be here, perhaps hiding in the shadows, when Carlton came in.

She had to prevent his entering the house. In a few minutes, the dogs and the hunters would be here. Locked outside, Dennis would not be able to escape them again.

The front door stood closed. She reached it breathlessly and threw the heavy bolt into place. Then she leaned weakly against it, trying to calculate the time it would take Carlton and the men to reach here. From upstairs, the dogs had sounded close, less than a mile at the most.

Just a few minutes then, she thought. She could go to the upstairs windows and watch for them, and when she saw them, she had only to yell down, to warn them.

She had started for the stairs when a sudden thought stopped her cold. The locked door would not keep Dennis from entering the house. In his own room were the windows he had broken open earlier, which he would surely remember. There was nothing to prevent his coming in the same way he had left.

She remembered the gun then, but it was still in the den. She ran, trying to make as little noise as possible. The gun was on the table where she had left it. She scooped it up and was back into the hall in a second, running for the stairs. She had reached them and was nearly to the first landing, taking them two at a time, when she heard the clatter of a chair being knocked aside in the hall below. It was followed by that less than human snarl she remembered so well.

She turned at the landing, grabbing the banister for support. He was at the bottom of the stairs, starting up. They both stopped, and their eyes met. She saw nothing but hatred and malice in his. He would not hesitate this time to kill her. She thought of the distance to Susan's room and knew she could not reach it before he caught her. There were other rooms closer, but she did not know which of them were locked and which unlocked.

Dennis snarled again and came up another step. The light fell on him. He looked even more ghoulish than before. His clothes were in shreds, his hair tangled and matted. He was covered with blood. Some of it was his own. She tried not to wonder about the rest.

She lifted the gun, aiming it straight at his chest. 'Dennis,' she said, hating her voice for quavering as it did. 'Don't. I'll shoot.'

He took another step. His eyes never left her face. She could not tell whether he even heard her voice.

Suddenly she remembered what Carlton had told her about the charms. Dennis thought he was a werewolf. He might believe the charms could stop him.

'Dennis,' she said, speaking more loudly. 'The bullets are silver. They have been blessed by Saint Hubert.'

He seemed not to hear. He came another step, then another. The distance between them was shrinking. Her hand shook as she tightened her grip on the pistol. He came closer. She thought she could smell the decay of the forest. Her face was damp with sweat.

He ignored the gun completely, and finally she realized what he had known all along, that she would not shoot him. She could not bring herself to pull the trigger. Monster though he might seem, he was human still. She had known him as a man. She had talked to him. He had told her he thought she was a good person. At least one time he had spared her life. She could not bring herself to shoot him.

Somewhere close at hand, voices shouted, and the dogs howled, a veritable cacophony now. There was a sound at the front door, and a violent pounding.

Carlton's voice called, 'Gaye, open up, it's us.'

The pounding stopped Dennis in his advance up the stairs. He looked down, toward the front door, expecting his brother to burst in, but now, as the door remained closed, he seemed to realize that it was bolted. For the moment, at least, his pursuers were locked out.

And a moment was all he needed. He turned back to Gaye, grinning monstrously, and began once more to ascend the stairs toward her.

She found her voice at last. 'Carlton,' she screamed with all the power of her lungs, 'he's in here!'

She raised the gun and threw it with all her strength into the hideous face grinning at her. Then, with a broken cry, she turned and ran up the stairs.

She heard him behind her, his breath a knell of terror. Her feet seemed leaden. She thought she had never moved so slowly. Something caught at her blouse, but the fabric tore away.

Susan had heard her. She burst into the

hall ahead of them. 'Gaye,' she began, and then screamed as she saw what pursued her.

Gaye hadn't the breath to tell her to go back inside, to lock the door. All of her strength was concentrated on lifting one foot, then another, again, again. Her heart pumped frantically, her breast felt as though it would burst. Susan's screams rang in her ears, over and over, and all of it seemed like a film playing in slow motion.

He had her at last, his clawing hands gripping her arm, then her waist. She stumbled, rolling upon the floor, and he was over her. She was in his grim embrace again, once more she saw his teeth bared, sinking down toward her throat, but she had no strength left this time to fight him away from that precious vein. She could not even pray. She felt his mouth at her throat, felt the hard touch of his teeth. She waited for life to leave her.

But it did not. Suddenly, curiously, she realized that he was not moving. He was a dead weight, crushing her down. And then Carlton was there, dragging him away from her, seizing her in those wonderfully protective arms. In his hand was the very gun she had thrown at Dennis. It brushed against her arm, and it was warm. She had not even heard the shot fired, so complete had been her terror.

* * *

It was a splendid morning. Craywood had never looked lovelier. The sky was nearly as blue as Carlton's smiling eyes, the sun only a little less golden than his hair. She watched with affectionate pride as he fitted the last of their luggage into the car.

She turned to Susan. 'Sure you won't change your mind and come along?' she asked.

'My darling little sister, you're still a goose,' Susan said, laughing. 'You're the only one in the world who would invite a third person along on a honeymoon.'

Gaye laughed too. She was happy to see Susan in such good spirits. 'I suppose you're right,' she said.

Carlton joined them, slipping an arm

possessively about Gaye's waist. 'Ready?' he asked.

She nodded and returned his quick kiss. 'Yes.'

'Sure you'll be all right here?' he asked Susan.

'Of course. The Stoddards are taking care of everything. And I'm still fond of Craywood, despite all that's happened. And, Carlton, thank you, but remember if you ever change your mind, it's still your home.'

'Thanks, but no thanks,' he said, taking a last look at the house. 'I'm glad you like it. I never did.'

'Neither did I,' Gaye agreed.

They said goodbyes and she and Carlton were on their way at last. She waved to Susan until they had pulled onto the road and were out of sight. Then she leaned comfortably back in the seat. They would be in San Francisco for dinner. Tomorrow they would arrive in Los Angeles, and then . . . but she couldn't think that far ahead, she was too filled with happiness in the present moment.

She stole a glance at Carlton. He

looked happy too, happier than she had ever seen him. She remembered how he had gazed at her in that moment when they were pronounced man and wife. It was the greatest joy of her life, seeing for one moment that look of love.

Not every moment had been so happy. From time to time she saw the shadows pass over his face, and she knew he was remembering, as he would remember for years to come, that awful moment when he'd had to shoot his own brother.

'But that,' he told her again and again, and firmly, 'is where you're wrong. He wasn't my brother anymore. He wasn't even human.'

She pushed aside the thoughts that accompanied that one. She had listened, dazed, as the men talked of that awful chase through the woods, in pursuit of a beast wilder and more savage than any of them had hunted before. One of the dogs had actually caught up with Dennis. Carlton was right, no human could have done what he did to that poor creature, but still she grieved for what he had been, and might have been.

'Hey,' Carlton said, glancing over at her. 'Not so serious.' He reached for her and pulled her across the seat, against him.

In a minute he said, 'That's the border. The Cray property ends here.'

Gaye looked at the fence separating the Cray lands from the neighbouring property. Craywood was truly behind her now, and before her . . . she sighed and snuggled happily against her husband.

THE END

We do hope that you have enjoyed reading this large print book.

Did you know that all of our titles are available for purchase?

We publish a wide range of high quality large print books including:
Romances, Mysteries, Classics
General Fiction
Non Fiction and Westerns

Special interest titles available in large print are:
The Little Oxford Dictionary
Music Book, Song Book
Hymn Book, Service Book

Also available from us courtesy of Oxford University Press:
Young Readers' Dictionary
(large print edition)
Young Readers' Thesaurus
(large print edition)

For further information or a free brochure, please contact us at:
Ulverscroft Large Print Books Ltd.,
The Green, Bradgate Road, Anstey,
Leicester, LE7 7FU, England.
Tel: (00 44) **0116 236 4325**
Fax: (00 44) **0116 234 0205**